# BLACKSTONE RANGER CHARMER

Blackstone Rangers Book 2

## ALICIA MONTGOMERY

# Also by Alicia Montgomery

Daughter of the Dragon

Shadow Wolf

A Touch of Magic

Heart of the Wolf

## THE BLACKSTONE MOUNTAIN SERIES

The Blackstone Dragon Heir

The Blackstone Bad Dragon

The Blackstone Bear

The Blackstone Wolf

The Blackstone Lion

The Blackstone She-Wolf

The Blackstone She-Bear

The Blackstone She-Dragon

## BLACKSTONE RANGERS SERIES

Blackstone Ranger Chief

Blackstone Ranger Charmer

Blackstone Ranger Hero

This is a work of fiction. Names, characters, businesses, places, events, locales, and incidents are either the products of the author's imagination or used in a fictitious manner. Any resemblance to actual persons, living or dead, or actual events is purely coincidental.

## About the Author

Alicia Montgomery has always dreamed of becoming a romance novel writer. She started writing down her stories in now long-forgotten diaries and notebooks, never thinking that her dream would come true. After taking the well-worn path to a stable career, she is now plunging into the world of self-publishing.

 facebook.com/aliciamontgomeryauthor

twitter.com/amontromance

bookbub.com/authors/alicia-montgomery

## Chapter 1

Gabriel Russel woke up that early spring morning with an urge. Urge to do what exactly, he wasn't sure. All he knew was that he was terribly hungry, and there was only one thing that could satisfy him.

His inner lion, usually the one to protest when he wanted to get up from bed, nosed at him in an attempt to hurry him up. Somehow it knew where they were headed, and seemed to want to get there sooner rather than later.

"So, chipper today, huh, buddy?" he told the lion. It only chuffed at him. "All right, all right."

Not many shifters talked out loud to their animals, but he and his lion had always been tight. Maybe because growing up, he'd felt lonely, and it was always there for him. Most people might have thought he was crazy—after all, growing up in a household with five siblings meant he was never alone. However, there was a loneliness that came with being the youngest *and* the only male in the family that few people would understand.

Springing up from bed, he headed straight to the bathroom to get ready for work. Contrary to popular belief, it didn't take hours for him to do his hair. Perhaps it was magic or just plain luck that his shoulder-length dark blond hair was easy to manage and seemed to come out looking perfect when he got out of bed in the morning. Of course, if anyone asked his sister, Giselle, she would say it was because she had ingrained in him the importance of good hair care products. In any case, on days he worked, he usually kept his hair tied back as the first time he went on patrol, he ended up with sticks, dirt, and leaves in his hair, which neither he nor his lion appreciated.

Work didn't start until nine, so that meant he had time for a bite of breakfast before he had to make the nearly one-hour drive up the mountains to the Blackstone Rangers Headquarters. So, after getting dressed in his khaki uniform, he grabbed his hat and headed down to the garage. Though most of his fellow rangers lived up or nearer to the Blackstone Mountains for convenience, he simply preferred his modern loft in South Blackstone. From there, he was near almost everything in town, plus, he liked the collection of shops, cafes, and restaurants that had been popping up around the growing area.

It only took him fifteen minutes to get to his destination – Main Street—and in particular, Rosie's Bakery and Cafe. As always, the smell of fresh pastries hit him with a nostalgic note. This was one of the places he'd go to with his father when he was still alive. Howard Russel would bring him here, and they would sit together in a booth, just the two of them, away from the chaos of the house. Those memories with his dad would be ones he would treasure forever.

In the last few weeks, however, coming in here gave him a different feeling. He couldn't quite put his finger on it, but it was as if he needed to be here, like this morning. After his father had passed, Gabriel would come to Rosie's maybe every other month or so, and on Howard's birthday.

But now he was here three or four times a week. Not that it

was a problem burning all those calories; he was a shifter, after all, and his job involved a lot of physical activity. Rosie gave him strange looks, but didn't question him on why he was here so often. Honestly, even if she did ask, he wasn't sure he could tell her because he didn't know himself. He only knew that he had to be here, not to mention, those new pies Rosie had been serving were irresistible. Just thinking of them made his mouth water.

"Good morning, Gabriel," Rosie, the owner of the cafe, greeted. As usual, the seemingly ageless fox shifter was clothed in a vintage dress, her vibrant red hair pinned up in curls around her head.

"Good morning, Rosie my love," he replied. Most people thought he was a shameless flirt, but he'd known Rosie since he was a kid, so there was no malice there, just deep affection for the older woman who had been serving Blackstone's best pies for nearly three decades.

"First one here, as always." Rosie gestured to the dining room. "Go ahead and sit anywhere. I'll grab the coffee, and you can tell me what you want."

Whistling as he walked over to his favorite booth, he sat down and glanced at the large display of pies near the back. Rosie's had a huge glass counter that featured over a dozen pies every day. Ever since he was a kid, he'd had a standard order: A slice of cherry, a slice of pecan, and a slice of lemon meringue, extra whipped cream. However, recently, he'd been adventurous with his choices.

As Rosie approached, coffee pot in one hand, he opened his mouth, but the older woman beat him to it.

"Our special flavors of the day are frozen pink lemonade, toasted coconut macadamia, and Andouille and Gruyère cheese breakfast pie," she rattled off. "I assume you want one of each?"

"Thank you, Rosie," he said. "And maybe a slice of cherry,

for old times' sake." It had been Dad's favorite, after all.

Rosie laughed. "All right, kiddo. Be with you in two shakes of a fox tail." After filling the empty mug on the table, she sashayed back to the kitchen.

Gabriel drummed his fingers, anticipation thrumming in his veins as he thought of the new pies. For nearly all his life, he'd ordered the same thing. Sure, Rosie would try a new recipe every now and then or there would be stuff that went in and out of season, but mostly, the place served the basics—apple, cherry, blueberry, key lime, chicken pot pie and the like.

But ever since these new flavors had been offered, he couldn't get enough of them. It was like a taste of heaven—the flavors bursting on his tongue was like the music of angels. They were better than anything he'd had before. The specials changed frequently, but even if the flavors were repeated, he would still order them. Those pies had almost become an obsession. The one day he came late after a shift and they ran out, he nearly threw a fit. It was like he'd been jealous someone else was enjoying those treats instead of him.

"Here you go, kiddo." She put four plates in front of him. "One pink lemonade, toasted coconut, breakfast, and cherry with extra whipped cream."

"You're the best, Rosie," he said, greedily eying the food in front of him. His inner lion, too, licked its lips.

"Looks like you need some privacy here, so I'll leave you alone now," she said with a chuckle, then waved as she sashayed back to toward the display counter.

Gabriel reached for his fork and dug into the breakfast pie first. His eyes rolled back into his head. *God, where have you been all my life?* The pastry was flaky and buttery and melted right in his mouth while the sausage, herbs, and cheese blended together in perfect harmony. His lion, too, was rolling around in ecstasy.

He took a bite of the two other pies and they were just as amazing, if not better. The cherry pie, too, was great, and though he hadn't had it in a while, he could swear it was even better than before. He had numerous memories of sitting here with Howard after he picked Gabriel up from school, talking about his classes and friends or nothing at all. He keenly felt the loss of his father, but even more than that, being here brought back all the good things he'd remembered about Howard before his life had been tragically taken in that plane crash along with his mother, Geraldine.

He swallowed the pastry and took a gulp of the coffee, washing it down. His lion was clawing at him, as if it wanted him to do ... something. Like it had an itch it couldn't scratch.

*Can't this wait, bud?* He was only halfway done with his meal.

It shook its head. *Now,* it seemed to say, its nostrils flaring.

But what did it want?

Putting the fork down, he glanced around. There was only one other table occupied, and Rosie was in front of the counter, wiping down the display case as another employee was taking out the apple pie to serve it up. Behind the counter was the door that led to the kitchen. As his gaze focused on the small round window in the door, he could have sworn he saw movement behind the glass.

The lion's head perked up.

*What?*

It pointed its nose toward the door.

*There?*

It nodded, shaggy mane shaking furiously.

Gabriel knew he shouldn't ... but he was already on his feet and striding toward the kitchen door.

"Sir?" someone said behind him. "Sir, you can't go back there."

His heart hammered wildly in his chest as he placed his hand on the door.

"What the—Gabriel Russel, get away from there—"

He ignored those words as blood roared in his ears. Something made him push the door open and stepped inside to see—

*Nothing.*

The kitchen was empty.

*What the hell is wrong with you?*

His lion protested with a yowl, then lifted its head to sniff the air. It smelled like butter, flour, pastry, and sugar, plus something else in the air he couldn't quite name. Something sweet and seductively exotic.

"Gabriel?" Rosie dashed into the kitchen, hands on her hips. "What in the world are you doing in here?"

"Huh?" What *did* he do? "Er, sorry, Rosie." He scratched at his head. "Didn't, er, sleep much last night. I'm still a zombie, and the caffeine hasn't quite kicked in."

Rosie looped an arm through his. "How about I refill your mug, then?"

"Uh, yeah, sure." As the fox shifter gently led him out of the kitchen, he glanced back at the door as it swung close. A strange feeling came over him, like an emptiness that he never realized was inside him. *Huh.*

Shaking his head, he allowed Rosie to bring him all the way back to his booth. "Thanks, Rosie my love," he said.

"I'll get you that coffee, kiddo. It'll fix up whatever's ailin' you."

His lion once again protested.

With a last glance back at the kitchen door, he couldn't help but feel like there would be nothing that could help fill this void that had somehow buried itself in his chest.

———

Gabriel didn't go back to Rosie's again after the day he barged into the kitchen. His lion didn't like that very much, but with winter behind them and spring in full bloom, he was just too busy. As a Blackstone Ranger, his work involved protecting the mountains and the forests in the area, but also, the people and shifters who came to visit, since it was a park. With the snow melting on the more popular paths, the mountains were busy which meant every one of the rangers had to be on alert for hikers or campers in distress, or even shifters who may have gotten too overconfident in their abilities and needed rescuing.

But aside from that, being deep in the forests meant he could avoid—or ignore—calls from certain people and blame it on the lack of reception. Even now, as he drove to Main Street after working overtime, his phone started ringing the moment it pinged the nearest cell towers.

Glancing at the screen, he saw the caller ID flash his oldest sister's name and blew out a breath. Genevieve was the last person he wanted to talk to right now. He knew what she wanted, but he was too tired to deal with her.

When the call went to voicemail, he let out a relived sigh, which was short-lived because his inbox now started blowing up. Checking the name of the sender, he groaned audibly. *Vicky Woolworth.* He'd rather talk to Gen and get a root canal and an appendectomy all at the same time than deal with Vicky. She was, as they said, twenty pounds of crazy in a five-pound bag. While he'd broken up with her years ago, she'd pop up every now and then. He had to keep blocking her and change his number whenever she got a new number or account, but that didn't seem to stop her from trying. *Looks like I have to call my cell company again.*

As he stopped at the light, he turned his phone off, glad for the silence. Today was supposed to be his day off, but he got stuck working overtime after helping search for a lost panther cub who had wandered away from its mother. His plan had been to sleep in and meet J.D. and Anna Victoria at Rosie's after they did wedding stuff. Instead, he had to shower at work and drive straight to Rosie's. When he got there, Damon was already seated at one of the booths.

"Hey, Chief," he greeted as he slid into the seat across from Damon. "Girls aren't here yet?"

Damon Cooper, who was his best friend and boss, shook his head. "Probably running late. Rogers filled me in about last night. Good job finding that panther cub."

"Yeah, she was pretty rattled, but once we got her back to her mama, everything was fine."

"I appreciate you guys staying and getting it all handled," he said.

"Of course, man. You know you can trust us for stuff like that." He patted Damon on the shoulder. "You're gonna be a married man soon; can't leave the Mrs. waiting."

At the mention of marriage and the Mrs., Damon's face lit up. "Jeez, I can't believe it's really happening."

Gabriel chuckled. "It definitely is." And he was glad for his best friend. If anyone deserved happiness with a mate, it was Damon, especially after all the shit he'd gone through. When he returned after being discharged from the Special Forces, Damon had been a shell of who he once was. Therapy and time had helped, but he had been driving himself into the ground with work and keeping all those feelings locked up. When he met his mate, things had changed—and for the better. "So, speaking of which—your bachelor party."

Damon groaned. "No. I don't want one."

"Ah, c'mon man!" Gabriel pleaded. "You only get married

once, which means I only get to be your best man once. Besides, this is your last night of—"

Damon shook his head. "You don't understand. I don't need a 'last night of freedom', because as far as I'm concerned, the day I met Anna Victoria, she became mine, and me, hers. Besides, my bear would never allow me to even look at another woman."

Gabriel didn't quite understand the concept of mates—no one really did. It was just one of those things that shifters talked about, but couldn't explain. Most shifters didn't even meet their mates. His own parents weren't mates. But apparently, from what he'd heard over the years, mating meant a special bond tied you to another person for the rest of your life.

Frankly, it sounded like a bad deal, after all, Gabriel pretty much already knew what was in store for *his* future. That's why he was determined to enjoy his life now, while he was still free.

Lately, however, seeing how happy Damon was, he couldn't help but wonder how it would feel to have another person who was the other half of your soul.

*Ridiculous*, he thought with a mental shake of his head.

His lion, however, mewled in disagreement.

"Morning, kiddos," Rosie greeted as she walked over to them, coffee pot in hand as usual. "What can I get ya?"

"Just the coffee," he said with a nod as Rosie filled the empty mug in front of him.

"And the specials for you?" Rosie asked Gabriel. "We have chocolate almond, cantaloupe, and bacon with egg."

"You got it," he said.

He and Damon chatted while waiting, but as soon as Rosie came back with their food, it was like his friend wasn't even there. He stopped listening to Damon drone on about butterfly populations or some shit, and concentrated on the delicious-smelling feast in front of him. *What was it about these pies?* He often wondered if Rosie put some kind of drug in them to make them addictive, though only he and his lion seemed to be unable to resist.

He quickly ate all the pies, with Damon rolling his eyes as he demolished them. His lion licked its lips, wanting more.

"They're here," Damon announced out of the blue.

Looking toward the door, he saw Anna Victoria and J.D., his other best friend, walk into the restaurant. As they always did, Damon and Anna Victoria instantly locked eyes, and it was like no one else existed in that moment.

A strange rush of envy passed through Gabriel. His lion, too, felt it and let out a whine. *Stop being such a pussy*, he told his animal. It had been doing that lately, whenever he was around the two.

"Everything go okay?" Damon asked as he made room for Anna Victoria on his side of the booth.

"Move," J.D. groused at him. "I want to be next to the window."

With a roll of his eyes, he got up to let her into the booth. J.D. had been one of his best friends since grade school, so he was used to her demeanor. She'd always been one of the guys— not fussy with her looks or clothes, but fiercely loyal, which was why he liked having her as a friend. Most people thought she was dating him or Damon. Gabriel had always thought she was pretty—even if she always dressed in oversized T-shirts and baggy jeans or overalls—with her messy blonde hair and hazel eyes, but they'd known each other so long, it would seem incestuous to date her now.

"Hey, ladies," Rosie greeted as she came over. "Do you know what you want?"

"I hope you didn't finish all of the special pies, Russel." J.D. nodded at the empty plates in front of him.

"They might have one or two left," he said. "Rosie my love, I gotta tell you, that cantaloupe pie was amazing."

Rosie chuckled. "Is there any of the new pies you don't like? You're here a couple times a week now. People might start talking."

"There's just something about them ..." He stared at the plates, still puzzled. "They all smell so good and taste heavenly. Like I've never known what food was like before."

"Well, I'll be sure to tell my girl you like her food."

"Girl?" His lion's ears perked up at attention. Rosie had mentioned the first time that she had a new employee making these pies. Why hadn't he ever asked before? He swung his head back to the kitchen door. "So, your employee ... is she still here?" he asked as his heart began to thud in his chest.

"Temperance?" Rosie's auburn brows knitted together. "Maybe. She doesn't usually leave until one or two but—oh, scuse me, kiddos." She nodded at the new arrivals waiting by the door. "I'll get your order in as soon as I seat them."

*Go. Now.*

As if in a trance, he got to his feet, pivoting toward the kitchen. His lion roared, pushing him to move faster until he crashed through the kitchen door.

There was someone shouting behind him, but he couldn't hear the words. He stood there, unable to move as his gaze fixed on ... *her*.

The woman was bent over the large table, dark brows knitted in concentration as she pushed out dough on the surface with a rolling pin. He could only see part of her face as she was facing sideways. However, she must have just realized he was staring at her as she lifted her head toward him.

As their gazes met, a strong feeling smashed into him. It felt like being struck by lightning, burning the edges of his nerves.

*Mine.*

And at that moment, his world turned upside down.

# Chapter 2

*No, no, no!*

This was not how it was supposed to happen.

In fact, this was not supposed to happen at all.

Temperance Pettigrew had been careful all these months, making sure she stayed inside the kitchen all the time, but especially when *he* was here.

He could never see her. Could never see her *face*.

She'd been so vigilant about keeping out of sight, watching him from behind the tiny window through the kitchen door, that holding onto the fluttering in her chest as he ate each slice of her special creations. Wanting, hoping ... but staying far, far away.

And the other day had been too close of a call. She couldn't help but watch him through the glass window, but then he stood and started walking toward her, and she knew she had to get away before he saw her. So, she dashed back to the pantry and hid, her heart hammering in her chest as she waited for him to leave.

He didn't know her. Never could know her. But she knew him.

How could she not? All the waitresses whispered and giggled when he was around. *Gabriel Russel.* How many times had she whispered the name to herself, said it out loud when she was alone at night?

Handsome didn't even begin to describe him. When Rosie told her a few weeks ago that she had a "fan," she was curious and looked out of the kitchen door window. Then she saw him.

Dark blond hair that glinted like bronze when sunlight hit it. A face like an angel. She didn't know what color his eyes were, but now she knew. Blue like the sky on a clear morning.

But what was he doing back here?

"I ..." She backed away, turning her face away from him. "You shouldn't be here!"

He advanced toward her, and she retreated. That didn't seem to deter him as he continued moving, which in turn made her keep going backward until her butt hit the sink.

"You ..." It was a single word, but the timbre of his voice made every hair on her body rise.

She tucked her body in further, face turning away from him. "Please." He couldn't see. He could never know. "Please don't."

"I thought I was going crazy. I knew there had to be a reason ... and now I know." He reached out to her, but when she shrank away, he dropped his hand to his side. "What's wrong, sweetheart?"

Her throat burned even as a thrill went through her at the affectionate nickname. "You need to go."

"Go?" He chuckled. "Why—"

"Gabriel Russel!" came a hiss from behind them. "What the hell are you doing?"

Temperance hoped he would turn around, and she could make her getaway, but Gabriel didn't move a muscle. His imposing presence should have scared her, but it didn't. *God, he was so tall and large.* She'd only seen him from far away, but having him here, mere inches away from her, he seemed even larger than life.

Not knowing what else to do, she peeked around his impossibly wide chest, making sure to keep the right side of her face hidden. She met the eyes of the woman standing in the doorway, instantly recognizing her as Gabriel's companion who often came here with him. A stab of jealousy hit her chest, and she turned away.

"Are you keeping that poor girl—"

A growl rattled from Gabriel's chest, and she jumped. Oh, she had heard about shifters—heck, all of the staff here except her was a shifter—but they didn't exactly talk out in the open about it. She knew Gabriel had to be one, too, and her curiosity piqued, wondering what he was.

*No! Stop wondering. He's not for you.* She had to get out of here.

"Look at me," he said in a low voice that brushed over her skin like velvet. "Why are you hiding from me?"

A vice-like grip tightened in her chest. There was no escape now.

But there was one way to get out of this mess.

*Just get it over with.*

Slowly, she turned her face up to him, her body instinctively tensing. Ready for the reaction. As their gazes met, everything went in slow motion.

His mouth turning up at the corners.

Then stopping halfway.

Sky-blue eyes widened.

And there it was.

The expression of horror on his face.

*Why did I think he would be different?*

Surely by now, she was used to that look—the disgust that

came just before pity when they saw the horrible burn scars on the right side of her face.

When she met people for the first time, they gave her that *look*. In the last eight years, she'd learned to shrug it off and move on. But somehow, coming from him, it was worse, like the first time she'd seen the extent of the damage herself.

If he was disgusted with what he saw now, then she couldn't imagine how he'd react if he saw the real extent of the damage.

Unable to continue being in his presence, she ducked away from him and then dashed toward the employees' exit. Rosie would not be happy that she didn't finish the day's work, but right now, she just couldn't be here. Her chest felt like it was going to cave in on itself, and if she didn't leave, she would have a breakdown.

The fresh air outside as she exited the building helped her to breathe, and somehow, she made it to her car. Quickly, she got inside and started the engine, thankful that she at least kept her car keys and wallet in her pockets. However, she was still wearing her apron, and her face and hair was still dusted with flour. The first thing she would do when she got home was take a shower.

It was a miracle she got home at all without crashing, as her hands were still shaking as she put the key into the door of her trailer. It was a thirty-minute drive from Main Street to the Sunshine Woods Mobile Home Park, but it was cheap, and her beater car managed the commute every day. Shutting the door behind her, she made a beeline for the shower, stripping her clothes off and pulling the pins out of her hair as she walked through the single wide.

The cold water felt cleansing as it blasted at her, but the tightness in her chest remained. Even as she closed her eyes, she couldn't erase the memory of Gabriel's expression when he saw her scars.

Water washed her tears away, but they continued to flow. Somehow, even after all these years, the hurt felt fresher now than it ever did before. She thought escaping her past would make it all go away. After all, starting fresh out here in Colorado meant there would be no reminders of Chicago. No reminders of the poor inner-city neighborhood where she grew up, of the various apartments and motels she shared with her mother and stepfather. And of course, the tragic event that scarred her for life and made her feel so worthless. Her self-esteem so crushed that she let someone isolate and abuse her because they gave her a morsel of affection she'd been craving all her life.

"It's not your fault," she said aloud.

Therapy and getting away from all of it helped a lot. But, oh, there were bad days, like today, that made her feel she would never truly forget or be free of the past. Not when she wore those reminders on her body.

Stepping out of the shower, she wrapped a towel around herself. As she passed by the sink, she froze. Normally, she didn't bother to stop and look at her reflection, but an urge made her stop. Maybe she was turning into a glutton for hurt or because she couldn't possibly feel any worse that she already did, but something in her made her want to confront her scars.

Slowly, she lifted her head to see the reflection in the mirror. When she had met other burn survivors the first few years after it happened, she knew it could have been worse. Some of them couldn't even hide their scars as it covered and discolored their entire faces or bodies, while she could easily hide them with the right hairstyle and clothes. Her eyes, lips, and ears were left intact, but webbed skin covered most of her cheek, and there was a patch of scalp behind her ear where hair couldn't grow. Her entire right shoulder and arm were covered in patches and scars that extended to just below her fingers. It was where most of the skin grafts were applied to ensure she would regain functionality and reduce the pain.

Her physical therapist helped her recover and even suggested she take up some kind of hobby to help the skin stretch and regain elasticity. That's when she discovered baking, which not only helped her physically but also mentally. She finally found something she was good at, something that she could be proud of. But then, when she thought things were looking up, it seemed life was only setting her up for the next disaster.

Unable to keep on staring at herself, Temperance whipped her head away and dashed out to the small bedroom. She grabbed her robe from the hook on her closet and put it on, then used the towel to dry her thick, dark hair. She kept her locks long as it was easy to style it to hide the right side of her face and neck, while long-sleeved shirts hid the rest.

Satisfied that her hair was dry enough, she meandered out to the combination living–kitchen room and put the tea kettle on. The single wide trailer was small, but she kept it clean and added a few pieces of decor to make it more homey, like the large Monstera plant in the corner, a lamp and reading chair, plus new throw pillows on the worn couch. It wasn't luxurious, but she loved it—loved being free, loved the independence of being able to do anything she wanted, whenever she wanted.

The kettle whistled, so she dropped a teabag into a mug and poured the hot water into it. After allowing it to cool for a minute, she grabbed the mug and then settled into her reading chair. Truly, she loved her life now; the last three months living in Blackstone had been an improvement over the last twenty-five years of her life. She was so thankful to get out of her last situation and that her boss at the bakery she worked for back in Chicago understood why she had to leave. They'd even referred her to a friend who ran a pie shop who was looking for help.

That's how she found herself in Colorado. Blackstone was a nice town, not that she had any time to see it. Her hours were from five in the morning to one in the afternoon. After that, she went straight home and read or watched TV, then fell asleep after dinner so she could do it all over again the next day. Her life had a routine; it was boring, but at least it was *her* life.

A knock on the door shook her out of her thoughts. Who could that be? *Probably those people from that church again.* When they came last week, she'd been too polite to tell them to leave her alone, so she accepted the book they offered and nodded when they said they'd be back. The book still lay on her kitchen table, untouched.

The knocking became insistent, so with a deep sigh, she got up, grabbed the book, and walked over to the door, yanking it open. "Look," she began, shoving the leather-bound tome forward. "You can take this—" Her heart stopped as she looked up into sky-blue eyes.

How long she stood there—mouth hanging open, saying nothing, book slammed up against his chest—she wasn't sure. But it felt like an awfully awkward, awfully long time.

He flashed her a smile that made him look even more handsome.

*Oh my God, he has dimples*, she groaned to herself, because of course he did. When the good Lord showered the world with all the good-looking genes, his parents must have gone outside with buckets in their hands.

"Uh, hi," he said. "Nice ..." He glanced around, his gaze immediately dropping to the statue guarding the front door of her trailer. "Nice gnome."

## Chapter 3

G abriel wanted to smack himself in the head. *Nice gnome? Smooth, Russel.* Real smooth.

But he didn't know what to do or say because how were you supposed to talk to your *mate*?

Shock was an understatement to describe how he'd felt at that moment when his lion recognized her as his mate. It roared at him to claim her. Even as she backed away from him, it only excited that raw, primal part of him.

But then he sensed real fear in her—and that just wouldn't do.

He needed her, to see her, know her. Why was she afraid of them? Why did she hide behind her dark mane of hair? His lion couldn't understand it.

When she turned her face to him, he was immediately struck by her clear hazel eyes. Light green with flecks of gold. He could stare at them all day, watch the light play in them. Wondered how they would look when she was happy. Or filled with desire while she was pinned under him.

Then he realized why she was turning away—those webs of scars on her cheeks. Burn scars likely, and he was suddenly filled with sadness because his mate must have endured so much pain. He could only imagine what it was like, and all he wanted to do was reach out and hold her and tell her it was all going to be okay. Wanted to shield her from anything else in the world that could hurt her.

But then she ran away. From him.

*Why?* His lion roared with fury and confusion.

And frankly, he couldn't figure it out either. Nor could he figure out what to say to her, so he decided to just continue with the absurdity that was slowly becoming his life. "Um, so, your gnome ..."

"Huh?"

He cocked his head at the garden gnome next to the door.

"You mean, Fred?" she asked.

"Fred? That's his name?" he asked incredulously.

"Is there a problem with Fred?"

"No—I mean, I was thinking he would have some kind of whimsical name. Like ... Mr. Peablossom or some shit like that."

"I've never really thought of it." She crinkled her nose. "He just seemed like a Fred."

"Have you always had Fred with you?"

"Kinda. I, uh, took him from my last house in Chicago, and he came here with me."

"So, you're from Chicago, huh?" he asked. "I've never been, but I heard they have good pizzas."

"Wait a minute ... How did you find me?"

There it was again; the fear in her voice. He could almost taste it in the air, and it made his lion mewl in distress.

When he didn't answer, her dark brows snapped together. "D-did Rosie tell you—"

"No!" he immediately denied. "She wouldn't do that—not to you. I have my ways."

Rosie had been furious with him for scaring her away.

"Gabriel Russel, what have you done?" she had fumed when she marched into the kitchen and realized Temperance was gone. "You scared my best employee away."

"I'm sorry," he had said. "But she's mine."

"Yours?" J.D. had asked.

"What are you saying, Gabriel?" Damon chimed in. Gabriel didn't even realize he and Anna Victoria had joined them in the kitchen.

"She's my mate."

Rosie had stood there, shocked. "I had no idea."

"Please, Rosie," he had begged. "Tell me where she lives. I need ... I need to talk to her."

The fox shifter had hesitated. "I can't do that. You know that would be violating her privacy." She blew out a breath and cocked her head slightly toward the row of employee punch cards next to the clock by the door. "But I'm going to turn around and leave the kitchen, so I won't see you doing anything you're not supposed to, like looking at the addresses printed on those cards."

"Thanks, Rosie," he had beamed.

It had been easy enough to find her card, since Rosie had mentioned her name, and the cafe didn't have a lot of workers. Temperance Pettigrew. Sunshine Woods Mobile Home Park was listed on the address line but no house number, but that would be enough. Hell, he'd knock on every door in Blackstone if that's what it took.

Thankfully, he only had to knock on five trailers before he found her.

"What do you want?" she said now in a quiet voice.

*You*, every cell in his body screamed.

His lion roared in approval.

Cool it. *She was human*, he reminded himself and his lion.

She didn't have an animal to tell her that he was her mate. "I just want to talk."

"To me?" she asked incredulously.

"Yes."

"But why?"

How was he going to explain it? "Er, can we start from the beginning? My name is Gabriel. Gabriel Russel."

"I know who you are."

"You do?" Now he was intrigued. He had known virtually nothing about her until this morning, except that she made the best goddammed pies he'd ever tasted. But she had known his name all this time? Why did she never come out to talk to him?

"Th-the girls at Rosie's talk about you all the time," she said in a wilting voice.

*Great.* He knew his reputation preceded him sometimes, and at this moment he wished it hadn't. As far as he knew, he hadn't slept with any of the waitresses there, but up until a few years ago, he'd been the wild child of Blackstone. Somehow, he had to convince her that he wasn't that person anymore. And that from now on, no other woman would matter to him except her.

"Temperance ... may I come in? So we can talk?"

"I don't think that's a good idea."

"Why not?" he asked, irritated. She flinched at his tone, and he felt like shit. "Sorry. I didn't mean to be rude." Unsure what to do, he raked his fingers through his hair. "Why did you run away?"

"W-why would I stay?" She swallowed audibly. "I knew you were ... you were ..." There was a pause as she took a deep breath. "I know what I look like, okay? It's not a pretty sight. I'm used to people thinking I'm repulsive."

"What?" He couldn't hold back the rage in his tone. His lion, too, roared in anger. "You think I was repulsed?"

"Weren't you?" she challenged.

He wasn't the type of man who was at a loss for words, but right now, he couldn't think of anything to say. *How did I miss it?* How did he not notice how she instinctively turned right side away from him the moment he burst in? Even now, her body was angled away, and a curtain of hair covered her scars. She thought he had been looking at her in disgust? Her, his *mate?* How could he ever think of her as not perfect in every way?

He opened his mouth to deny it, but she put a hand up. "Please, just leave me alone. Whatever it is you want to say to me, I'm sure it's not that important."

Not important? His lion shook its head in denial unable to process the idea that she was his mate as not important?

There had to be a way to fix this. But how? "If you give me one minute—"

"Please!" The distress in her voice made him sick to his stomach. "Please. Leave."

His lion was fighting him, clawing at him. It didn't want to leave their mate. What if something happened to her? Was this place even safe? What was the security like here? Were there any rival males around to claim her before they did? If anything happened to her while they were away, the lion would never forgive him.

However, he had to let his rational, human side win out this time. In time, she would come to understand. She was obviously too distressed right now. "All right." Putting his hands up, he stepped away. She didn't even give him a second glance as she shut the door in his face.

*Fuck.*

The lion inside him let out a sad yowl at her rejection. *Sorry, buddy*, he consoled. But we're not giving up.

The animal's ears perked up, as if saying, *we're not?*

*Nope. No way.*

Squaring his shoulders, he put on a determined expression. He was Gabriel Russel. *And you're a lion, king of the jungle*, he told his animal. They were not backing down.

*But how am I supposed to claim her?*

With a sigh, he stepped back, then his gaze dropped to Fred. His nose wrinkled at the ugly thing—the garden ornament had obviously seen better days. Its long, pointed cap had probably been bright indigo at some point, but it was now a faded color between gray and blue. The end of its nose was chipped off, however the maniacal grin on its face was intact, mocking him. It seemed to say, *Well, well, isn't this ironic?*

He snorted. *Yeah? Keep laughing, Fred.*

It was time to put on the full Gabriel Russel charm treatment. And heck, if he couldn't sweep her off her feet, then maybe he didn't deserve her as a mate.

# Chapter 4

The alarm buzzed at three o'clock in the morning as it always did, and Temperance reached over to shut it off. Her mind was still in that half-asleep, half-awake state as she went through her morning routine.

After getting dressed, she grabbed her purse and keys, then headed out the door. She turned to lock it, but froze as she felt the hairs on the back of her neck stand on end.

"Don't be scared. It's just me. Gabriel."

Her keys dropped to the floor. The memories of what happened yesterday flooded into her sleepy brain. *It wasn't all a dream, after all.* As she bent down to pick her keys up, he was instantly there. Problem was, he was faster than her, and they knocked their heads together when they both bent down.

"Ow!" she exclaimed, rubbing at her temple.

"Sorry," he said sheepishly. "I've been told I have a hard head." His offered hand contained her keys. "Here you go."

"Thanks." She swiped them from his palm. "I—what are you doing here?" On instinct, she turned her right side away from him, despite it being dark out. Did she hit her head too hard, and was she seeing things now? *No wait.* That was *after* he announced that he was here.

"Er ..." He shoved his hands in his pockets. "About that—"

"I thought I told you to leave?"

"You did," he said. "Yesterday. And you didn't say anything about not coming back."

Without turning her head, her eyes peeked up at him. Was he serious? The absurdity of this entire conversation—and his presence here—made her mind snap back to reality. She glanced at her watch. It was past three thirty already. "Look, I should get to work." Brushing past him, she headed straight for her car. However, she couldn't help but feel his eyes on her even as she got into her vehicle.

*I will not look back, I will not look back.* But it was an impulse she couldn't control. Turning her head, she looked back at her trailer and found he was gone. *Good.* Though a small— very small—part of her was disappointed.

When she started her car engine, however, she heard a second, much louder, engine behind her roar to life, and the headlights reflecting in her rearview mirror nearly blinded her before they dimmed. Muttering a curse under her breath, she put the car into gear and drove out of the trailer park.

The vehicle behind her followed her out, but then she reasoned that there was only one road out of there. Then she turned into the main road and onto the highway on-ramp, and still the car was there. It was too dark to see what it was, though it seemed like some kind of truck or SUV based on the lights. The vehicle stayed behind a good distance, but she couldn't help but feel it was following her. And though she didn't want to admit it—she could guess who was driving it.

*If it was Gabriel, then it didn't mean anything.* After all, Seventy-Five was the main highway that cut through Blackstone, and everyone took it to get around town. And even now, the exit ramp she took was the one that everybody used to get to Main Street.

As usual, she was the first one to pull into the rear parking lot of Rosie's. As the main pie baker, she had to get up really early to prepare all the regular pies and special orders, as well as the new pies she came up with every day.

Temperance wasn't quite sure where her ideas for the original pies came from—they just seemed to pop into her head. She would be kneading the dough or watching TV or taking a long, hot shower, and then it would just come into her mind. Various ingredients and food jumbled together in her head, a mishmash of ideas and thoughts that would form the basis of her new creation.

*Almond butter with a dash of cinnamon.*

*Green tomato salsa.*

*Pork arepas with a cornmeal crust.*

After writing down the idea in the notebook she took with her everywhere, she'd work on the ideas once all the pies were ready. It usually only took two or three tries to get a recipe right. Most of the original creations were hits, but there were a few that outsold them all so those were rotated on a regular basis which helped when her creative juices ran dry. There were a few ingredients she wanted to work with today, but as she got out of her car and walked toward the restaurant, new ideas popped into her mind.

*Golden honey. With a touch of lavender.*

*Blueberries with cardamom.*

Better get those down on paper before—

"Temperance, what's wrong?"

"Mother of—" She nearly jumped out of her skin as Gabriel's deep, velvety voice interrupted her trance. "What are you doing here?"

He appeared in front of her as if from out of nowhere. "You seemed like you were in a daze."

"I—" Warmth flooded her cheeks. "I was just thinking. And are you following me?"

"I had to," he said, looking sheepish. "I mean ... your car doesn't look safe."

Her cheeks grew hot again, but this time, of embarrassment. Looking back, she saw the shiny brand-new red Jeep parked behind her rusted out Kia. "Sorry I can't afford any better. But if you're done insulting me, you can go now."

"I didn't—" His lips thinned, and he raked a hand through his dark honey-colored hair. "*Christ*." He muttered something under his breath. "That's not what I meant. I just didn't want your car breaking down in the middle of the highway and then having some guys jump you or something."

"Seriously? Where do you think we are, South Side? I've been going to work by myself for the last three months just fine."

"Hey, Blackstone can be dangerous," he countered. "I mean, we've had some trouble around here, you know."

She blew out a breath. "I'm here. You can go now." Walking around him, she strode to the back door and slipped the key into the knob. A prickly feeling crawled over the back of her neck, and when she turned her head, she startled. He was right behind her. "Do you mind?"

"Not at all," he said, his sensuous mouth curling up into a smile.

Warmth pooled in her belly, but she ignored it. "I can't let you in. It's employees only. If you want to come in, you'll have to wait until we open."

"That's fine. I'll stay out here and make sure no one disturbs you."

While part of her wanted to continue to argue with him, those pies weren't going to bake themselves. "Do as you please," she grumbled, then walked into the kitchen. *He'll get bored. Or tired.* And then he'll leave and never come back. She told herself that's what she wanted and, that's how it should be.

Rolling her long sleeves up her arms and pinning her hair back, Temperance set about her morning routine, going into automatic pilot. However, in the back of her mind, she couldn't help but wonder if Gabriel was still out there. Surely, he had better things to do than just wait there, guarding the door from supposed robbers or muggers or whatever the heck he thought was coming to break in here while she was baking.

At around seven thirty, she heard Rosie and Bridgette come in through the front door as they usually did. Bridgette stayed out in the dining room so she could get it ready for the day, while Rosie came to the kitchen to help her. The older woman knew Temperance was self-conscious about the scars on her face and arms, so she made sure no one else came in here while she baked.

"Good morning, Temperance," Rosie greeted as she grabbed an apron from the hook in the corner.

When Temperance first came to Blackstone for this job, Rosie had been doing most of the baking by herself. After over thirty years, she realized it was time to slow down, which is why she hired Temperance. Rosie has shown her what to do that first week and basically left her to her own devices after that, coming in only just before opening to help her finish up the morning's pies.

Temperance took out the first batch of apple pies and placed them on the counter to cool. "Rosie, I'm so sorry for running out on you yesterday," she began, biting her lip. "I just ..."

"It's all right, sweetie," Rosie assured her as she came over and patted her on the arm. "So ... is everything okay?"

"Yeah." Why was Rosie looking at her weird? "Shouldn't it be?"

"Er." Rosie cleared her throat and played with the pearl necklace around her throat. "I mean ... is Gabriel ... did he find you?"

Her cheeks warmed, but then again, of course Rosie would know. She nodded, unsure what to say.

A small gasp escaped her lips. "And?"

Her brows knit together. "And what?"

"Did he say ... anything?"

"I ..." Where would she begin? "He said he wanted to talk, but I told him there was nothing to say."

"Oh." Rosie sounded deeply disappointed, and she shook her head. "I know it's not my place to say anything, but if you need to talk—"

"I'm fine." She turned around and grabbed two of the pecan pies that were waiting to be placed into the oven. "He's just ..." With a sigh, she put the pies in, then shut the door quickly.

"Are you sure you're okay, Temperance?"

Jolting out of her thoughts, she pasted a smile on her face. "I'm fine, really. We should finish up those cherry pies," she said, nodding at the empty shells.

"Of course," Rosie began. "I'll get the filling and—Gabriel?"

*Gabriel?*

Then the hairs on the back of her neck prickled. Turning toward the door, her breath caught in her lungs as she saw him poking his head in the doorway, his dark bronze hair glinting with gold highlights in the early morning sun. It almost hurt to look at how handsome he was.

"Hey, Rosie," he greeted. "I just wanted to say goodbye."

Rosie's auburn brows snapped together. "Goodbye?"

"Yeah." Gabriel scooted inside. "I brought Temperance to work this morning—"

"Followed me," she corrected.

"*Followed* her to work," he conceded. "To make sure she was okay."

Rosie's eyes widened. "You followed her this morning ... does that mean you stayed with her? All night?"

"What?" Mortification filled Temperance, from the top of her head to the tips of her toes. "No!"

Gabriel frowned, then shook his head. "When I, uh, glanced at her time card yesterday, I saw she comes in real early. And it's dark out at that time, and I didn't want her driving alone," he said. "So, I went to her place and followed her here. Then I stayed outside to make sure no one bothers her."

"Huh." Rosie and Gabriel exchanged glances, then she turned to Temperance. "I never really thought about it, but maybe I should be making sure you were okay here by yourself so early in the morning."

"It's all good," she said, miffed. "I've been fine for the last couple of months. Blackstone is much safer than where I used to work in Chicago. I've only gotten mugged once in my life."

"Once?" Gabriel exclaimed. "What do you mean *once*?"

She could have sworn she heard a snarl from him. "I was a teenager, flipping burgers at a fast-food place," she said. "And I was out late when my manager asked me to stay after shift to clean up. It's no biggie, I just gave up my purse when he waved a gun at me."

"No biggie?" His hands stiffened at his sides. "What if something happened to you back then? And if you never made it here and—"

Rosie cleared her throat loudly. "Gabriel, doesn't your shift start soon? It's a long drive up the mountains."

He looked conflicted, but nodded. "Yeah, I should go." Reaching into his pocket, he offered a piece of paper to

Temperance. "This is my number. Call me if you need anything."

"I won't need you for anything," she scoffed.

His mouth flattened, but he grabbed her left hand and placed the scrap into her palm. The contact with his bare skin made gooseflesh rise on her arms, but she ignored it.

"I'll see you later, Temperance," he said, flashing her another smile.

"I—what do you mean, later?" But it was too late. He'd disappeared, the door slamming shut. Unsure what to do, she tossed the scrap of paper in the trash.

Feeling Rosie's stare boring a hole in her back, she turned around and swallowed hard. "I can explain." Actually, she couldn't, because she was even more confused now.

"It's none of my business, sweetie," Rosie said as the corners of her mouth tugged up. "But I have to say, this is going to be interesting."

Temperance groaned and wiped a flour-covered hand on her forehead. *Maybe if I'm lucky, I won't see him again.* She did *not* like the way Gabriel made her feel when he was around. She wanted to squash all those butterflies in her stomach and ignore the way the backs of her knees tingled when he smiled at her. What would it be like to see that every day? To have him smile for her, and her only? And maybe spend all her days and nights with him.

A small, internal voice scoffed at her, and she shook her head.

*Get to work,* she told herself. Work would be her balm, a way to forget about the past and her non-existent future with Gabriel.

Hours passed, and the work of getting dozens and dozens of pies ready helped Temperance focus. At least it did until lunchtime, when she heard a knock at the back door.

"Temperance Pettigrew?" the young man said as she poked her head out of the door.

"Yes?" Using her apron, she wiped the sweat from her brow. "That's me."

"I have a delivery for you." He held up a brown paper bag emblazoned with the local Chinese restaurant's logo on the front.

"I didn't order anything," she said.

The teen shrugged. "I'm just doin' my job, lady." He pushed the paper bag at her. "It's all paid for, even my tip. But the guy on the phone who ordered it was pretty clear about making sure I get this into your hands."

She stared at the bag, slack-jawed. Did she dare wonder who the "guy" was?

"I gotta go back and make more deliveries, lady," he said. "Just take it, okay?"

Not wanting to keep him waiting, she took the bag. The tempting smell of fried rice made her stomach growl. "Uh, thanks." Usually she skipped lunch or grabbed a quick bite to eat at the cafe down the street. Having food brought to her was a treat.

*I shouldn't.* She worried at her lip with her teeth. *I can't accept this.* But the food smelled amazing, and the thought of throwing away a perfectly good meal made her stomach twist. Growing up poor, she never wasted a single scrap of food.

With a deep sigh, she turned around and closed the door behind her, then walked over to the counter in the corner. When she opened the bag, she groaned. *Oh my God, this smells amazing.* There were several boxes of food inside, enough to feed at least four people.

Unable to resist, she opened up all the boxes and grabbed the fork that came in the bag. Everything tasted as good as it smelled; maybe even better. There were two kinds of fried rice, noodles in a savory brown sauce, steamed dumplings, chicken with cashews, and beef drowning in a scrumptious gravy that made her want to weep. At one point, Rosie poked her head into the kitchen, glanced at the food but said nothing, though there was that mysterious smile on her face again.

After she finished eating, she put the remaining boxes away, vowing to eat the leftovers for lunch the next day or share it with her coworkers. Feeling full and satisfied, and with the rest of the day's orders and pies done, she could now work on her own recipes.

When she worked on her new pies, she went into a trance-like state. Nothing could distract her as she grabbed ingredients, mixed them together, rolled out the dough, and put the finished pies in the oven. Strangely, her inspiration for today wasn't even something she had thought of beforehand or written down in her notebook. Instead, she let her nose, taste buds, and instincts honed from years of baking tell her what ingredients and techniques to use.

The timer on the oven dinged, letting her know it was done. Looking through the small window, she saw the crusts were perfectly golden brown, so she carefully set the two pies out onto the counter.

"Temperance ..."

Glancing up, she saw Rosie standing by the door. "Yes?"

The older woman took a sniff. "Something smells delicious. Like, really, really good." Her gaze dropped down to the two pies on the counter. "Something new?"

She nodded. "Yeah, want to try?"

"Of course."

Temperance grabbed the knife and plates, then put a slice on each. "Here you go."

Rosie took a forkful of one. "Oh. Wow," she said through a mouthful of pastry. Then, she took a bite of the other. "Huh."

Her eyes rolled back. "What is this? This is probably the best ones you've made yet."

"Thank you." She stared down at the two pies, making a mental note to write everything down before she forgot it. "That first one is golden honey with lavender. And the other one is blueberry."

Rosie took another bite of the blueberry. "But there's something spicy and exotic in it."

"Cardamom," she said.

"Huh, I never thought those two would go together, but they do. So," Rosie began, "you seem to be inspired this morning. Anything you need to tell me?" When she blushed, Rosie laughed. "I'm just teasing you." She finished both pie slices as Temperance looked on. "Wow. We definitely have to put that on the menu."

"I'll work on them tomorrow," she said proudly.

"Now, why don't you go home?" Rosie urged. "You looked exhausted, sweetie."

Glancing up at the clock, she saw it was nearly four o'clock. Usually she was out of here by two at the latest, but she wanted to spend extra time on making those two pies perfect. "I feel exhausted. Would you and Janine mind cleaning up?"

"Not at all, sweetie. You earned it."

After taking her apron off, washing up, she waved goodbye to Rosie and headed out the door.

Soon, she was back home, pulling up to the front of her trailer. As always, she was dead tired, but there was something satisfying about finishing a day's work. As she trudged up to her front door, she suddenly stopped.

"Oh no. No, no." This was a joke, right? "Gabriel, what did you do?"

Sitting in front of her door was a humungous bouquet of red roses. It was so big it nearly engulfed her tiny porch. Bending down, she picked them up, taking in a whiff of the floral perfume from the perfect buds. Each rose was the size of her fist with not a single blemish on them, so they must have cost a fortune. Taking the card attached, she opened it up.

*Pretty roses for a pretty lady.*

*G.*

It was hard not to feel the giddiness bubbling up inside her, but it didn't take more than two seconds for it to burst and deflate.

*Pretty?* a voice inside her sneered. *Surely that was a mistake. He can't mean* you.

That small voice was something she hadn't heard in a while. Her self-confidence hadn't been great even before the fire, but certainly, it had been left in tatters when her life imploded right before she came to Blackstone.

That self-doubting voice somehow seeded inside her head, one that always told her that she was nothing—a worthless waste of space who would never amount to anything. Coming here, getting away from it all quieted that voice, but now it was threatening to haunt her again.

Shutting her eyes tight, she ignored the twisting in her gut. Did Gabriel have some sort of vision impairment? Or was this all part of an elaborate joke? How far was he going to take it?

With a deep sigh, she put the flowers down on the floor, her gaze meeting Fred's. That painted smile on his face seemed consolatory today, and she reached over to pat him on his faded cap. "Thanks, Fred."

He seemed to be the only male she could trust right now which was pathetic considering he was made of plaster and paint. Still, he was her only friend out here. The garden gnome used to occupy a spot in the garden of her previous home, and the day she walked away from that place—and her entire life—

an impulse made her pick up the statue. She strapped Fred to the front seat of her car and drove off, never looking back.

*This couldn't be.*

There was no way she was going to fall for a charmer and his empty promises.

"Not again," she whispered, swallowing the lump in her throat. Finally, she'd found peace and a quiet life in Blackstone. She wasn't going to risk all that for just another handsome face.

———

The familiar alarm buzzed at three in the morning, and once again, Temperance reached over to the bedside table to turn it off. Her morning routine was so ingrained that she was still half asleep by the time she yanked the front door open.

"Why did you leave my flowers out here?"

"Jesus, Mary, and Joseph!" She jumped back as she nearly ran smack into a wall of roses. Taking a deep breath, she massaged her chest. "You're here *again?*"

Despite the frown on his face, Gabriel still looked handsome and surprisingly fresh as a daisy, as if he got up every day at three o'clock. *Or maybe he rolled out of bed looking perfect,* she muttered to herself. It totally wasn't fair.

"You don't like roses?" He held up the bouquet. "That's okay. What flowers *do* you like?"

"I—" She shook her head. "What are you doing here?"

"You're headed to work right? I didn't want you to go by yourself."

"Go by my—" With an exasperated sound, she brushed past him.

"Hey, where are going?"

Whirling around, she faced him again. "I told you, I don't

need to be brought to work like some kid on the first day of kindergarten."

Though she walked fast, he quickly caught up to her. "Hey, are you mad at me? For the flowers? Or for coming here?"

Was she mad? She wasn't really sure how she felt, except maybe confused and tired. "I just don't know what you want from me."

"Nothing," he said. "You don't need to give me anything back."

It felt like there was an "except" coming there, but she didn't really have time to play games today. Or any day.

Ignoring him, she got into her car, started the engine and drove away. A few minutes later, there were headlights tailing her on the highway. Blowing out a breath, she continued driving on until she reached the parking lot behind Rosie's. She had barely opened the door when she heard his voice.

"Temperance!"

But she ignored his call and scrambled into the restaurant, slamming the door in his face. With a deep sigh, she leaned back against the door and closed her eyes. *What was his deal?*

"I'll just be out here until eight," the muffled voice came through the door. "In case you need me."

A thrill ran up her spine at his words, but she pushed those confusing emotions aside. *If I ignore him, he'll go away eventually*, she told herself as she got ready for the day.

Of course, that was wishful thinking on her part. At lunchtime, another food delivery came, this time from the Italian place down the street. Rosie had raised a brow at her, but remained silent. Then when she came home, there was not only a huge bouquet of sunflowers sitting on her porch, but a small crown of them around Fred's head.

*How about these?* the note on the card began. *You're as bright as sunshine.*

Her stomach flip-flopped, and for a brief moment, she felt excitement at those words. But she didn't even need that negative inner voice to break her down. *This just can't be.*

*But he keeps coming back. That has to mean something, right?*

The truth was, her instincts were so damaged, she didn't know what to think.

Gabriel wasn't acting like any man she'd ever met or been with. But she knew his type.

*Tony was exactly the same.* They were all alike, all those shallow, handsome men who only wanted one thing from a person. Well, in the case of her ex, he wanted two things—get her into bed *and* support his lazy ass for a year while cheating on her with multiple women.

Getting herself out of that situation had not been easy and had cost her what little she had, but she did it. When she hightailed it out of Chicago, she told herself she would never let herself be fooled by another sweet-talking handsome man. She'd learned her lesson the hard way.

Would Gabriel show up on her doorstep again? She wasn't going to take the chance, so she set her alarm an hour early the next day. Seeing nothing but darkness out on her porch should have made her feel relieved, but there was a strange disappointment brewing in her. But she ignored it, even as she pulled up to the empty parking lot behind the restaurant.

By the time Rosie came in, there was still no sign of Gabriel. *That's good,* she thought. Maybe he got tired of following her around.

"Everything all right?" Rosie asked as she put her apron on.

"Huh? Yeah I'm fine."

"Then why is your egg wash bowl empty?"

She double blinked before looking down at the bowl and

brush in her hands. Apparently, she'd been brushing air on the crusts for about ten minutes. "Oh. Er ..."

Rosie sauntered over to the window and slyly glanced out. "No Gabriel today?"

"I wouldn't know," she said, reaching for an egg and cracking it into the bowl.

The older woman raised a brow at her. "When are you going to take pity on that poor boy?"

"I don't know what you mean."

The redhead chuckled. "Ooh, Temperance, you really don't know what you've gotten yourself into."

Dropping the bowl with a loud clatter, she turned to her boss. "No, I really don't. Maybe you could let me in on the joke, because I'm getting tired of it," she snapped. Suddenly realizing her outburst, she covered her mouth. "Crap. I'm sorry, Rosie."

Rosie clucked her tongue. "Oh, sweetie, no. I'm the one who should apologize." Walking over to her, she placed a sympathetic hand on her shoulder. "Maybe I should have told you."

"Told me what?"

"That Gabriel—"

The back door bursting open interrupted her as a large, fast blur rushed into the kitchen. "Rosie, where's—*you're here.*" His entire body froze, like someone had pressed pause on a movie.

She had never quite seen Gabriel like this before. He laughed, teased, and smiled, but the Gabriel in front of her now was like a completely different person. His entire body was tense, like a tightly coiled spring waiting to be released. Golden brows were drawn forward, and his eyes blazed like hot blue fire as they fixed on her. Slowly, he stalked toward her, and she couldn't help but feel like a gazelle trapped by a predator.

"Where were you?" His voice was tight, and his hands were balled at his sides.

"Here," she said matter-of-factly. "At my job. Where I am every morning."

"I came by your place, and you didn't come out at three thirty. So, I broke into your house—"

"You broke into my house?" she asked incredulously, anger making her step forward boldly.

"What was I supposed to do? You were gone!"

"But you didn't have to break into my trailer," she shot back. "Why the hell would you do that?"

"I was scared that maybe you hurt yourself," he said. "Then I realize your car wasn't in the driveway, and I thought maybe you didn't come home and that maybe you'd gotten into an accident or worse. Drove all the way to Blackstone Hospital to see if they had anyone of your description, and when the ER nurse said no, I went to the police headquarters—"

"What the hell?" *Was he serious?* "You thought something happened to me because I left my house an hour early to go to work?"

He let out a frustrated growl that made her shiver. "You could have been lying in a ditch. Or kidnapped or—" Cornering her, he hunched his shoulders forward. "Why the hell would you do that? Can't you see I only want to protect you and keep you safe?"

"Safe from what?" Gabriel had run around town looking for her? *This was crazy.* "The only thing I need protecting from is crazy stalkers like you. Were you dropped on your head as a child or something?"

"I swear, woman, you're going to put me in an early grave."

"Why do you care anyway? Why can't you just leave me be!"

"Leave you be?" He raised his arms in frustration. "How can I do that when you're my m—"

"*Gabriel Russel,*" came Rosie's stern voice from behind. The admonishing tone was enough for him to snap his mouth shut. She strode over to them, hands on her hips. "Out."

Gabriel's gaze flicked briefly at Temperance. "Rosie, I'm sorry for bursting in. Please, don't kick me out—"

She held a hand up and pointed to the door. "Wait for me out there."

Temperance would have been amused at how the tiny woman ordered him around despite towering over her by nearly a foot, but she was too confused. And maybe a little bit excited at the thought that Gabriel was worried for her.

*Wait, what?*

"Rose—"

"Wait. Out. There," Rosie ordered as she hooked her arm through his and dragged him to the door. Pushing him out, she slammed the door. "You okay?" she asked Temperance.

"I'm s-sorry, Rosie," she stuttered. "I don't know why he did that. Or why he's doing ... this." With a defeated sigh, she plonked down onto the nearest chair. "Is he playing a joke on me?"

"A joke?" Rosie chuckled and then shook her head. "Oh, sweetie. I realize now Gabriel has been going about this all wrong, but you really can't see it, can't you?"

"Can't see what?"

"To put it mildly, that boy is interested in you."

If it were possible, her jaw would have literally dropped to the floor. "In me?"

"Yes, you."

"B-but why?"

An auburn brow rose high. "And why not?"

"You're kidding, right?" Using her left hand, she gestured to her face and arm. "Because of this. Why would someone like him be interested in someone like me?" Saying it out loud made a knife-like pain stab into her chest, but maybe this was something she needed to hear.

"Oh. Sweetie." Rosie clucked her tongue. "Do you think Gabriel is that shallow?" She opened her mouth to say yes, but shut it when Rosie raised a hand. "You don't know him, Temperance."

"But I have eyes, and I can see." Her gaze dropped to her shoes. "Him and me? Can you imagine it?"

"Why, yes. I can."

She snapped her head up, and when she locked gazes with Rosie, she could see what she was totally serious. "That's nice of you to say, but he's him and I'm ... me."

"You mean, a kind, hardworking woman who's beautiful on the inside *and* out?"

"Rose—"

"Tut-tut." Rosie raised a hand again. "Hush now. Why can't you believe that Gabriel is sincerely interested in you? That he can see past your scars and see the real you?"

A sob burned at her throat. She wasn't even sure she knew who she was. The fire had left physical scars on her, then a terrible relationship afterwards had left emotional ones until she wasn't sure there was anything left of her.

"You might think that Gabriel is this perfect, handsome prince—and on the surface, that might be true which is why you're intimidated." Rosie said. "But there's so much more to that man, if you'd only give him a chance to show it to you."

A laugh bubbled up in her. Her, give *him* a chance? Was the world turning topsy-turvy now?

"Look." Rosie bent down in front of her and gave her hands a squeeze. "Let me go talk to him, okay? See if I can at least ... make him understand your hesitation and maybe get him to slow down. Oh, these shifter men," she chuckled with a shake of her head. "Felines are the worst of all, you know, always so used to getting their way. Especially lions. All bluster, and no subtlety at all. And overconfident to boot."

"L-lion?"

"Yeah." Rosie rolled her eyes. "King of the jungle and all that."

*Huh.* So, Gabriel was a lion. Somehow, she had a feeling about his animal, but couldn't quite say it out loud. But it made sense—he always moved with a languid, confident grace that projected he owned the room or any space he was in.

"I'll go now. Why don't you sit tight or take a break? If I think he's calmed down enough, I'll let you know, and you can decide if you want to talk to him."

"I—" But before she could protest, Rosie was already out the door. She blew out a breath, her body feeling like a deflated balloon.

The thought that Gabriel possibly *liked* her was still churning in her head. And right now, she just couldn't get it to process, like a dough that just wouldn't proof. What would she say to him if Rosie asked her to come out and talk to him?

She buried her face in her hands and let out a frustrated groan.

## Chapter 5

Gabriel's stomach dropped as the door shut in his face. His lion, on the other hand, roared in fury. How dare that little fox keep them away from their mate. If Rosie had been a male, the lion would have shown it who was boss around here.

*Can it*, he ordered his animal. Not that he thought it would ever harm Rosie, but they were both being pushed to the limit here. He'd had so many mood swings today someone might have thought he was on his period or something. The feeling of dread he had in the pit of his stomach the entire morning was slowly ebbing away, but it left him emotionally exhausted.

When she didn't come out of her trailer that morning by three forty-five, he had begun to get worried. After knocking on her door for several minutes, he got impatient and broke the lock. Then, realizing she wasn't in there, his mental state spiraled, and his lion wasn't helping as it pressed him to find her *now*.

*Why the hell didn't we check here first?*

His lion actually had the decency to slink away in shame.

Raking his hands through his hair, he paced back and forth, unsure what to do next. *I've ruined things*, he thought sadly. But he couldn't stay away from her, couldn't get her out of his head. Every moment of his existence pulsated with a need that he couldn't ignore.

"Are you calmed down enough?"

He halted, then whipped his head toward the door.

Rosie closed it and raised an auburn brow at him. "Gabriel Russel, what in the world is the matter with you?"

"I don't know, Rosie." Then tension in his shoulders lessened, but the pit in his stomach grew. "I messed things up, didn't I? She thinks I'm some kind of crazy stalker. I just ... I couldn't stay away, you know? I can't. When I thought that she might be in trouble, something in me snapped and—"

She clucked her tongue. "You overwhelmed her."

"I know, but I can't. I just ... I don't know what to do with a mate. I never thought I would find mine." A different uneasy feeling crept into his chest, but he ignored it for now because there was no use thinking about his family and Gen if his mate wouldn't even look at him right now. That was a whole different issue. "And now she doesn't want me."

"It's not that she doesn't want you, Gabriel." Rosie placed a hand on his shoulder sympathetically. "She just doesn't understand what's happening, being human."

"It would be easier if she was a shifter."

Rosie laughed out loud. "Lord, do you really think human and shifter females aren't similar? I thought you had more sense than that. Growing up, you never did starve for female attention, whether it was from that suffocating family of yours or all those women fawning all over you. Maybe it's time you did some of the chasing, Gabriel Russel."

"I know, I know," he said glumly. "I'm easy on the eyes." Rosie snorted but he continued. "I have a job. I look pretty hot when I'm in my uniform."

"And you're richer than sin," Rosie added.

He winced, not really thinking about that. "Then why doesn't she want me?"

"Gabriel, have you ever thought that perhaps those are the reasons she *doesn't* want you?"

"What?"

The older woman's lips twisted. "You're not blind right, you can see her scars?"

"Yeah, and so?"

"And so?" she parroted. "How do you think she feels about them?"

"Does it matter?"

"It does to her," she said. "It's part of her, something she has to live with every day. And you can't just ignore them—"

"I'm not." But Rosie's words made him think. Truly, aside from the fact that she must have been in incredible pain, those scars didn't matter to him at all. Obviously, it bothered Temperance a lot. "Do you know what happened?"

"Not the whole story." Rosie's tone lowered. "But you can't just ignore her scars. She's extremely self-conscious about them, and it's not just about how she looks. There's a deeper scarring there, one we can't see." She sighed. "Temperance is an amazing person—inside and out. You don't even know how lucky you are that she's your mate. But her confidence has been left in tatters by God knows what, and so, when you come in and start throwing your weight around, she won't believe you want her for her."

*Huh.* He'd never really thought of that. Of course not. His entire focus in trying to claim Temperance had been to *make* her want him back. Now he realized what he had to do was *earn* her. "What do I do, Rosie?"

"Talk to her. Show her you genuinely want her for her, and for God's sake, listen to the things she's saying *and* not saying. You're used to showing everyone your perfect side, but maybe what Temperance needs to see is your flawed, human side. Trust me, she'll respect you more for it."

"And what about us being mates? Should I tell her?"

"That's up to you, kiddo." Rosie patted him on the cheek. "You'll know when it's time." There was a sad smile on her face, and Gabriel wondered if there was any meaning behind it.

"Will she even talk to me?"

"She might be persuaded. Wait here."

Gabriel felt his body tense again when Rosie disappeared through the door. It seemed like an eternity passed, but he didn't dare look away. Finally, the knob turned, and the door opened slowly.

Temperance peeked her head out, then quickly turned away to hide the right side of her face. A pain plucked at his chest wondering if he had blown it with her. He thought they had gotten past the whole conversation about her scars, seeing as he'd told her he wasn't disgusted. Seeing her like this, skittish around him, made him realize his mistake—not only did he try to bully his way into her life, but he'd failed to make her feel safe and secure around him. And that just wouldn't do.

"Rosie said you wanted to talk to me?" she asked.

"Yes, but only if you want to."

She shrugged.

"I just wanted to say ..." He swallowed the lump in his throat. "I'm sorry about overreacting this morning. I should have checked in with you here. And ... and I should have sat down and talked to you." Sweat formed on his palms. "The thing is, Temperance ... I like you. I really, *really* like you." That didn't seem enough to convey how he felt, but he had to remember to take things slow.

One hazel eye looked up at him. "You do?"

"Uh-huh. There's no joke. No ulterior motives. When I

went crazy this morning, it was because I genuinely thought you were in trouble."

"B-but you hardly know me." She paused, her gaze lowering. "*I* don't even know you."

"All right then, we'll get to know each other," he began. "Let's give this a whirl. Ask me anything."

She blinked and turned her head slightly so both eyes snapped up to meet his gaze. "Now?"

"There's no better time." He smiled at her. "Go ahead. Ask me anything."

"Well ... tell me something about yourself."

Gabriel knew he could have told her a million things about himself—his favorite color, his job, about growing up. But the first thing he blurted out was, "I hate frogs."

"What?"

"They're slimy and gross and have these creepy eyes." He shuddered. "I can't stand them. When I see them, my chest starts to seize up, and I can't breathe."

"But don't you work as a ranger?" She nodded at the patch on his uniform. "That means you have to spend a lot of time outdoors."

"Believe me, I know the irony."

"But frogs are cute and harmless," she cried. "They're lovely, especially the colorful ones."

"Of course you'd love them," he grumbled.

"You can't stand them ... not even that puppet one on TV?"

While he took Rosie's advice to heart about showing her some weakness, he wasn't about to hand in his man card. "He's, er, all right. Especially when he sings and plays the banjo."

She laughed—a genuine, honest-to-goodness laugh that warmed his insides. Even his lion mewled happily, pleased to see their mate so amused.

"I don't understand," she giggled. "Why do you hate frogs? Did something happen when you were a kid?"

"I could tell you," he began. "Maybe ... over dinner?" Damn it, he'd tell her the story and endure talking more about those gross amphibians if she said yes. *Oh God, let her say yes.*

Her teeth worried at her lip. "I ... I suppose that would be okay."

"Is that a yes?"

"I—yes. But"—a frown marred her pretty face—"I can't stay out late. I need to be asleep by ten or else I won't be able to get up early for work."

Now *that* would be a problem, because he didn't get out until nine at night, but it wasn't impossible to fix. "I'll take care of it." Damon would understand. After all, he was mated himself. "It might take a day or two. Can I call you and arrange it?"

She nodded, and he handed her his phone so she could type her number in. "I'll call you right away." Then he winced. "I also called locksmith on the way here to fix your lock by the way. It'll be done by the time you're home."

"Thank you. I should get back to work now," she said. "Um, so I'll see you."

"See you, Temperance."

With a quick nod, she scampered back inside. He waited for one heartbeat before expelling a great big breath from his lungs. "Yes!" he exclaimed, as he high fived his lion. *We did it, buddy!*

His animal let out a howl of triumph. *Mine.*

"Um, not quite *yet*. But soon." He'd take her out on a couple of dates, and once she was ready to hear it, tell her they were mates, and then they could bond.

The lion titled its head, as if asking, *how?*

"Huh." He scratched his head. "I'm not sure." But he could figure that out later, or maybe ask Damon about it.

*Mine.* His lion huffed impatiently. *Mine.*

He shook his head. "It's not time yet," he said aloud. If he couldn't control his lion, they would scare her away, maybe for good.

*Doubtful,* his lion seemed to say as it rested its snout on its paws.

Gabriel snorted, then turned and began to walk toward his Jeep. "Trust me, buddy. We had a big win today." His lion had always been impatient, but he hoped just for this once, it would trust him and let him set the pace. "She's worth the wait." That, at least, they seemed to agree on. Now, to get back to HQ and work out their scheduling problem.

As he predicted, Damon was more than happy to hear things were progressing with Temperance.

"Congrats, man." Damon got up from behind his desk in his office at the Blackstone Rangers HQ and clapped him on the back. "Mates are a special thing, you know. Not all of us get a chance at meeting ours."

"I know," he said. "So ... what do I do to make sure the mating bond forms?"

The chief's dark brows drew together. "I don't really know ... I mean, for Anna Victoria and me, it just kind of happened. From what I've heard, it's different for each couple. But I think when you're both ready and open to accept it, you'll feel the bond form into place."

Gabriel scratched at his chin. That really didn't help, but he knew Damon wouldn't be holding out on him if he really did know the answer.

"You should spend time with her, get to know her," Damon added. "And get her to know you. Your animal already knows Temperance is your mate, but she'll need more convincing."

Good thing Damon had brought that up first. "Speaking of which ... I do have a little problem." He briefly explained

Temperance's schedule. "Anything you can do? I'm scared she's gonna get cold feet if I don't act soon," His lion paced, agitated at the thought. *Don't worry, buddy*, he reassured his animal. *We won't let that happen.*

Damon rubbed his chin with his thumb and forefinger. "My hands are tied scheduling-wise since I don't want to be accused of favoritism. But, find someone to swap with, and I'll approve it. Do what you need to do to win your mate over."

"All right, I'll ask around. Thanks, man."

Of course, he thought finding someone to swap shifts for a couple of days would have been easy, but it was more challenging than he'd anticipated since Temperance worked odd hours, so he might have to get two people to split shifts with. If he couldn't, that would mean he would have to take some unplanned vacations days—and he couldn't do that to Damon, especially with his wedding and honeymoon coming up.

The first person he had in mind was Daniel Rogers, who was easily one of the nicest and easy-going guys on the team.

"Sorry, Gabe," Daniel said when he asked him. "My parents just got into town for a visit, so I already have all evenings off. Maybe next week?"

His lion huffed brusquely. Next week would be too late, but he knew Rogers wouldn't have said no if it were possible. No one else he approached could do it either because they already had prior commitments or didn't have the hours he wanted off. There was only one person he hadn't asked yet, but he was absolutely Gabriel's last resort.

"Hey, Anders," he greeted the tiger shifter in the locker room. "Can we talk?"

Anders Stevens was flexing and admiring himself in the mirrors, completely unruffled by the fact that he was buck naked. Of course, shifters tended not to be self-conscious about nudity, though Stevens seemed to enjoy literally swinging his dick around for fun.

Anders put on a big smile and planted his hands on his hip. "Russel. Glad you finally came to see me."

"You are?"

"Yeah. Heard you were trying to swap your hours for the next couple of days. Do you have something important going on?" He placed his hands over his heart in a mock gesture of shock. "Frankly, I'm hurt you didn't ask me first."

That's because he knew he was going to pay through the nose for any favor from Anders. The man was an asshole. A lovable asshole, but an asshole nonetheless. "Well, can you do it?"

"Sure, man. What hours do you need?"

"I just need to be outta here by five p.m., and I can be back by five a.m." It would be tricky because all the shifts were nine to nine, plus it would throw off his own sleeping schedule. Not that he planned on doing a lot of sleeping if things with Temperance went right. "Or I can get Rogers to split—"

"Pshaw." Anders waved a hand. "Piece of cake." The tiger shifter always said he preferred the nine o'clock overnight shifts because it was a good excuse to hightail it out of a girl's bed once he was done banging her.

"Really? You can get Rogers to—"

"Like I said, piece of cake," Anders reiterated. "I'll take care of it. Now you can go polish the gold bars in your vault or whatever it is you trust fund babies need to do."

Gabriel rolled his eyes. However, this transaction had seemed entirely, suspiciously too easy. "All right, Anders, what do you want in return?"

"Damon's bachelor party."

Gabriel scrubbed a hand down his face. "Damon's already decided not to have one."

The other man crossed his arms over his chest. "Well, I guess that means you're going to make him *un*-decide."

"So that's what you want in return? You just want to make sure Damon has a bachelor party?"

"I want to plan the whole shebang." There was a gleam in his eyes that made Gabriel nervous. "And you'll pony up the cash to pay for it. And I want the works, Russel. Vegas. Presidential Suite. Private jet."

Gabriel grit his teeth. The money wasn't the problem, but it was getting Damon to agree. *He did say to "do what you need to do" to win Temperance over.* "All right, I'll work on it." He'd worry about getting Damon to agree *and* stop Anna Victoria from stringing him up by his balls later.

"Awesome." Anders turned back to his locker and sprayed himself with deodorant. "I'll run some ideas by you later. You won't regret this."

Somehow, Gabriel doubted it. But at least he got what he wanted. As he strode out of the locker room, he took his phone out and typed a message to Temperance.

*Was the lock fixed?*

The locksmith he called had already told him it was all done, but he wanted an excuse to start the conversation.

He knew not to expect a reply right away, but his stomach flip-flopped when he saw the dots pulsing on the screen indicating that she was typing back a message.

*Yes. Thanks for getting that done.*

*Well I did break it.* Sheepish emoji. *Sorry. Dinner to make it up to you?* Smiley face. *Pick you up at six?*

*Tonight? That's a little soon.*

He frowned. If only she knew how excruciating slow the whole dating thing seemed to him, especially when he wanted her to be his *yesterday*.

*Why not? Do you like Indian or French?* If she had come up

with all those pie flavors, that would mean she was a foodie, so he hoped he scored points by offering up exotic options.

*There's a French restaurant here in Blackstone?!?*

*Yeah,* he typed back. *A braserie opened in South Blackstone a couple days ago.*

*\*brasserie,* she corrected. *Sorry.*

He laughed aloud. *Baby, you can correct me all you want. So, yes?*

When dots didn't appear right away, Gabriel felt his lungs constrict. However, when the reply popped up, he found he could breathe again.

*Yes.*

"Hallelujah!" He raised a fist in the air and jumped for joy. His inner lion, too, roared in triumph.

"Whoa, Russel," Anders commented as he exited the locker room. "Let me guess, your sister said you could buy another Porsche this year?"

Normally he would have told Anders to fuck off, but instead, he laughed and clapped him on the shoulder. "I'll see you at five, Stevens," he said. "Oh, and by the way, I'm supposed to be on trash duty this week. Good luck with that."

Anders's face turned from smug to irate. "What the fuck? Trash duty? You didn't say anything about trash duty!"

Gabriel merely whistled as he walked away so he could start his shift.

"I want strippers at this party, Russel," Anders screamed at him. "The good kind."

But he ignored his friend's tirade, as he was walking on cloud nine in anticipation of his date with his mate.

The hours seemed to stretch into days as Gabriel went through his shift, despite the fact that he didn't even have to finish the entire twelve hours. By four thirty he was changing into his street clothes and driving down the mountain. He avoided both Damon and Anders, but he figured he'd sort out the whole bachelor party thing later; after all, he was about to embark on the most important date of his life.

After swinging by the florist where he picked up another bouquet, he drove straight to Temperance's house. It was just about six when he walked up and knocked on the door.

A bead of sweat formed on his forehead, and doubt crept into his mind. *What if she's changed her mind? Or she didn't want—*

The door opened. "Hey." As Temperance looked up at him, a shy smile on her face, all that doubt quickly dispelled.

"Hi," he greeted back. "These are for you."

"Oh." Temperance took the flowers from his hands. "Thank you."

God, she looked so beautiful. She wore a simple navy blouse and white skirt, while her long dark curls hung down one shoulder. Her hazel eyes seemed to glow, but when he caught her gaze, she quickly turned her right side away from him.

A flicker of annoyance pecked at him at the gesture. He longed to make her see that those scars didn't matter to him, but he didn't know how to do that exactly. But for now, maybe it was better to just not mention them at all.

"They're mums, I think," he said. "The flowers, I mean."

"They're gorgeous. Can I bring them along, or should I put them inside?"

"Just bring them, they'll be okay for a few hours." Truth was, he didn't want to wait a second longer. "I made reservations."

"Oh, okay." Stepping out of the house, she quickly locked the door. "And are we taking your car?"

"Yeah." He offered his arm. "My chariot awaits, my lady."

A pretty blush bloomed on her cheek as she looped her arm through his. This close, he finally got a whiff of her sweet, feminine scent, and it was enough to send a stab of desire through him. *Control yourself, Russel.* Despite his own needs, the last thing he wanted to do was act like a caveman around her.

He escorted her to his Jeep, opening the door for her and helping her up the step. Temperance was of normal height he supposed, though he still towered over her. Walking around, he slid into the driver's seat and started the engine.

"How was your day?" he asked as he maneuvered the vehicle out of the mobile home park.

"Long, but good." One light hazel eye peeked over at him.

"Mine too," he said. "But I'm happy it's done. My shift anyway."

There was a short awkward silence, then she swallowed audibly. "So, you like being a ranger?"

"It's a good job, I suppose," he said. "What about you? Do you like working for Rosie?" He glanced over at her.

"Yeah, she's nice." Temperance fiddled with her fingers on her lap.

They drove the rest of the way in silence, but he wasn't disappointed or annoyed; it was obvious they were both nervous. He himself felt so anxious about not making a mistake that he felt like a teen on his first date. Still, there was a simmering excitement bubbling underneath the surface, a nervous energy that had his lion pacing in anticipation. Soon, he slid into a parking spot inside the garage next to where the restaurant was located.

"Where did you hear about this place?" she asked as they

walked to the entrance of the restaurant which had a red painted sign that said *Brasserie Cannes*.

"I actually live near here," he said casually. "I walked by this place a couple weeks ago and saw they were opening soon."

"You live here?" she glanced around nervously. "It's, uh, a nice neighborhood."

"I suppose," he said with a shrug, then opened the door for her and followed in behind. "Good evening, I have a reservation," he said to the young woman at the station. "Russel, table for two."

"Let me check on that for you, sir," she began, then peered down at the electronic tablet in front of her. "Russel ... hmmm. Oh. *Oh no.*" She frowned, then looked up at him sheepishly. "I do remember taking your call, but I think we had a little glitch, because I can't find it." Panicked, she looked around. "I'm so sorry, Mr. Russel. Everything's so new and I just started here a few days ago. I can arrange something for you, but would you mind waiting by the bar for a few minutes?"

"It's all right," he assured her. "We can wait, right, Temperance?"

She nodded. "Of course."

"Oh, thank you," the hostess said, relieved. "This is my first time using this system and it's still buggy. Come this way please." She led them to the bar on the right side of the dining room. He ordered a beer for himself, and Temperance asked for a sparkling water.

"So," he began. "You said you moved here from Chicago? How do you like Blackstone?"

She seemed to tense when he first mentioned Chicago, but quickly relaxed when he asked her about Blackstone. "I love it here, actually," she said. "It's different. But there's so many things to love about this place."

"Like what?"

As she began to talk, he half-listened because he was too distracted at how close they suddenly were standing next to each other. Thank God the hostess had lost his reservation, because he wouldn't have had this chance to be so near her if they had been sitting on opposite ends of a table. This close, he could see the way the lights played in her eyes and watch her plump lips part when she spoke. That intoxicating scent of hers teased him as well, and he had to grip his beer glass tight to stop himself from acting on his need. *God, I hope I can at least get a goodnight kiss.* Being this near her and not touching her was driving him and his lion insane.

"... it's also so quiet," she continued. "Which I like. Back when I was working in the city, I heard car horns and sirens all day long."

"I should take you hiking up in the mountains," he said, taking a small sip of his beer. "It's real quiet there."

"I'm not very outdoorsy."

"Neither am I."

She giggled, her voice like bells. "Are you sure you're really cut out to be a ranger?"

Everyone who knew him before the rangers would be surprised too. "Yeah, but I only joined—"

"Gabriel Russel. Is that you?"

His entire body froze at the sound of that low, sultry drawl. *Motherfucker, not now.* Clearing his throat, he turned his head toward the source of the voice and then cursed a blue streak in his head when he confirmed who it was. "Hello, Vicky." *What the hell was she doing here?*

Vicky Woolworth stood inches behind him; her slick red lips turned up into a smile. "*Gabe.*" She leaned over to kiss him on the cheek. His lion bristled, not wanting to even breathe the same air as the lioness. "It's been a while. Why haven't you been answering my calls?" she asked with a fake pout.

*Maybe because I blocked your number and your social media accounts, you psycho?* However, he didn't want to make a scene. "I've been busy." He glanced over at the man beside her. "Hi."

"Oh, excuse my rudeness." She patted Gabriel on the shoulder. "This is my date, Tom Melnick. Tom, this is Gabriel Russel. We go *way* back."

"Tom," he nodded at the man as he took the offered hand. Melnick was tall, handsome, and by the look of his expensive suit and watch, very rich. So, in short, he was Vicky's type.

"Nice to meet you, Gabe," Melnick said as they shook hands.

"It's Gabriel," he corrected.

"Only I get to call him Gabe," Vicky laughed. "Oh, who's your ... friend?"

*Crap.* Turning around, he saw Temperance shrink away from them, anxiety rolling off her in waves. This really wasn't how he wanted this night to turn out. *Of all the fucking places and times Vicky could have shown up, it had to be tonight?*

"This is my date," he said, emphasizing the last word as he placed an arm around her. "Temperance Pettigrew."

Temperance flinched when his arm landed on her shoulder, but at least she didn't shrug it off. "Hello," she said in a soft voice. She didn't look at Vicky or Tom, but instead, kept the right side of her face and body away from them.

Vicky's perfectly shaped blonde brow rose high. "Pettigrew? Are you one of the Long Island Pettigrews?"

"I ..." Temperance shook her head. "No, I'm from Chicago originally."

"Really? Which part?" Vicky prodded.

"A suburb you probably wouldn't know," she said with a nervous laugh.

Vicky's nose wrinkled at the mention of the suburbs. "I'm sure I don't," the lioness said with disinterest.

"Don't you have a table?" Gabriel snapped at her. He was not going to play Vicky's games. Not anymore.

"We do, actually," Melnick said, clearing his throat. "Vicky?"

Flipping her long blonde hair over her shoulder, Vicky pasted a big smile on her face. "I'll see you around, Gabe."

As the other couple walked away, Temperance ducked her head and shook his arm off. "I need to use the ladies' room," she said before quickly scampering away, not even looking up at him.

Gabriel cursed inwardly. Downing his beer, he signaled the bartender for another one. Why he ever got involved with that crazy lioness, he didn't know. Maybe because he was young and stupid, and their families encouraged it.

The Woolworth's lineage was just as blue as the Russel's, and everyone had expected them to get married. But after a while, he realized that she was, indeed, a few cards short of a deck. Still, it took him a while to fully get rid of her. But every now and then, she popped up like a nasty rash. He usually shut her down quickly, blocking her and avoiding any places where she might show up.

He knew growing up what his purpose in life was as the only male in his family of notoriously matriarchal shifters. In the past few years, he'd managed to avoid it all, even rebelling with his choice of career. He could have his choice of cushy jobs in the Lyon Industries organizational chart, but he didn't want to be involved in all that, and for the most part, his sisters had left him alone.

But a few months ago, Gen started getting on his case about "family duty" and all that shit. Oh, he knew why his eldest sister had been calling and leaving numerous voice mails lately. Vicky sliding into his DMs and now bumping into her seemed suspiciously coincidental.

Minutes ticked by, and he realized he had finished his second beer already. *Where the heck was that hostess with that table?* On second thought, maybe it would be a good idea to find another place to eat.

"You're still here, Gabe?"

*Fuck.*

Whirling around, he fixed a neutral expression on face. "Don't you have a date you have to go back to?"

The corner of her lips turned up. "Why? Are you jealous?" Leaning over, she trailed her fingers up his arm. "You know it gets me hot when you are."

*Christ,* nothing had changed in in five years. Vicky was still a raging lunatic. "Don't start, Vicky." Wrapping his fingers around her wrist, he pulled her claws off. "And stop contacting me. Newsflash: when someone blocks your number and social media accounts, they generally don't want to hear from you."

"But we were so good together," she said with a pout, leaning forward to take up his personal space. A hand crept up his chest. "Surely, you don't want that weak little human? Are you just waiting to get her in the sack?" She scoffed. "She's a nobody. And those disgusting scars—"

"Shut the fuck up!" His lion, too, was seeing red at the insult to their mate. His hands gripped at her arms, trapping her against the bar with his body. "You're not even worth a fraction of her."

They stood there for a few seconds as he waited for her to push him away. Instead, she slinked her torso up against him. "I knew you still had it in you." Her gaze flickered to something behind him, and she smirked. "Oh, Gabe, we were always so good together."

He pushed off her and raked his fingers through his hair.

"What the fuck are you—" He froze, then whirled back to Vicky. "How did you know about her scars?"

Vicky smoothed her perfectly-manicured hands down her dress but didn't say anything.

A pit formed in his gut. "Where the hell is my table?" he barked as the hostess passed by them.

The young woman started, then hugged the menus she was carrying to her chest like a shield. "S-sir? I thought you changed your mind." She cocked her head at the exit. "Your date ... she left."

A murderous feeling crept into him as he put together what could have happened. "Goddammit! You planned this," he growled at Vicky.

Fear flashed in the lioness's face for a brief second. "Gabe! Don't you dare—"

Ignoring Vicky, he dashed out of the restaurant. "Temperance!" he called. There was a faint trace of her scent in the air, but there was no sign of her. However, the sound of a door closing and then a car driving away caught his attention, and he saw a car idling across the street. *Goddammit!* As the sedan pulled away, he thought to run after it, but he knew better. Besides, if Temperance had called for a ride, he already knew where she was going.

He sprinted to the car garage where he'd parked, then drove as fast as he legally could all the way to Temperance's house. His lion mewled in distress, not liking the fact that their mate ran away from them.

"I know, buddy," he said under his breath. "*Fucking Vicky.*"

She probably saw an opportunity when Temperance went to the bathroom and pounced on the chance to confront her, away from Gabriel. Lionesses could be ruthless like that. Plus, he could only imagine what she'd said to Temperance. But knowing his ex, it couldn't have been good.

He practically leapt out of the Jeep as soon as he got to her house, not even bothering to turn the engine off. "Temperance!" he called, rapping on her door. "Temperance!"

She didn't answer, but his keen senses could hear her moving around inside. His chest tightened, and his lion growled and snapped its jaws at the flimsy door. With his shifter strength and claws, he could tear that scrap of metal into shreds in seconds, but he would never do anything to frighten her.

"Go home, Gabriel," came the faint voice from the other side.

"Please, Temperance," he begged, desperation clawing at him as he braced his palms on the door frame. "We didn't even finish our date. Why don't I order us some food—"

"I'm not hungry. And I'm t-t-tired." Her voice seemed louder now, so he could imagine her just on the other side of the door, centimeters away from him.

"What did she say, Temperance? What did Vicky tell you?"

"N-nothing."

"I don't believe you. Open this door or I'll—"

"Don't make me call the police," she said. "*Please.*"

The hurt in her voice struck a chord in him. *What a fucking mess.* The moment Vicky walked into the restaurant; he should have insisted on leaving. That woman was hell-bent on destroying his life; she'd already tried five years ago.

Leaning his forehead on the door, he let out a long huff. He knew he could wait it out here all night. But she had work in the morning, and so did he, plus, Anders was already doing him a favor, so he didn't want to abuse the other man's good will by showing up late. "This isn't over, Temperance," he warned. However, only silence answered him back.

He knew he had to make her listen. But how? Seeing him with Vicky had probably shattered the already tenuous trust she had in him. And now she wouldn't even come out to see him and let him explain. *Maybe it was time to give up.*

As he pushed himself off the door, the grinning figure of Fred caught his eye.

An idea popped into his head.

*No.*

*Wait.*

*Could he ...?*

Well, as they say, desperate times called for desperate measures.

# Chapter 6

*Did you really think he would want you?*
      *You're delusional.*
*Why would he choose you over* her? *Or any other girl for that matter?*

*He's so out of your league. What were you thinking?*

Temperance bit her lip, as if that would make that voice of doubt go away. However, now that that voice had once again started to make itself home in her brain, it didn't want to leave.

She didn't move, only stared at her door, waiting. Only when she heard the shuffle of footsteps and the sound of a vehicle driving away did she allow herself to breathe. Trudging back to her tiny bathroom, she stripped and stepped into the shower, wishing she could wash off this whole day, too.

*It was better this way.* Better that she stopped acting like a fool before she got hurt. She'd been giddy the entire day waiting for six o'clock to arrive, primping and preparing herself for Gabriel, even managing to curl her hair so as to hide her cheek. She looked almost normal. Almost good enough to be standing next to Gabriel.

Oh, when she opened the door and he was there ... she

nearly chickened out because he looked incredibly handsome. He was dressed simply in khaki pants and a dress shirt that made his eyes look bluer. His long, bronzed hair looked perfect as always, and that smile on his face made her melt.

Everything seemed to be going well, despite the initial awkwardness. She was starting to feel more relaxed and confident around him. Even starting to open up to him.

And then *she* came along. Vicky with her perfect blonde waves of hair. Perfect heart-shaped face and nose. Perfect body and legs till Mexico. And perfect *skin*.

It was obvious Vicky and Gabriel had a past from the way she was so familiar around him. She was exactly the kind of woman that Gabriel should have on his arm. Even though Vicky was on a date with another man, that hot slice of jealousy in Temperance's chest wouldn't go away as she watched her and Gabriel interact.

Though she didn't really need to go to the bathroom, she had to get out of there. She was staring at herself in the mirror, trying to fix her hair which had fallen out of place when Vicky walked in, looking *perfect* in her designer dress and red-bottomed shoes, a cloud of expensive perfume in her wake as she walked behind Temperance and stood at the next sink over. When their gazes met in the mirror, the look of shock—and disgust—on Vicky's face was evident. Temperance realized she had her hair pulled back, and the scars looked even harsher under the fluorescent light of the bathroom.

The horror on Vicky's face, however, had dissipated, and a satisfied smile crept up on her lips. Temperance's stomach clenched at the silent communication the other woman seemed to convey—that she was obviously not worthy of Gabriel. Vicky didn't even think Temperance worth speaking to as she finished washing her hands and strode out of the bathroom confidently.

Yes, it was true what she said to Gabriel. Vicky didn't say

anything. She didn't have to; that look was all Temperance needed. And if that wasn't enough, seeing Gabriel at the bar, pressed up against her, was the final straw, and she high-tailed it out of there.

*But he followed you here,* a small voice inside her said.

*Maybe he didn't like it when a woman left him in the middle of the date,* she told herself as she shut off the shower. *Or he was trying to get me into bed too, and saving Vicky for later.*

As she dried herself off and changed into her pajamas, that seed of doubt that had planted in her grew even more. Why wouldn't it? It happened before, after all.

When she met her now ex, Tony, she couldn't believe a guy like him—good-looking, charming, with a hot body—would go for someone like her. Sure, it had been seven years since the accident that left her like this, but she hadn't had the confidence to even attempt dating. Tony had been a regular at the Wicker Park bakery where she worked as he was employed at the construction site across the street. Back then, aside from baking, she also had to work as a cashier, so he would come in and flirt with her when he got his coffee and breakfast in the mornings, eventually asking her out to dinner after a few weeks.

It had been a whirlwind romance, to say the least. She had been on cloud nine because he was the perfect boyfriend—attentive, romantic, and said all the right things. Perhaps him moving into her place a month after their first date had been a little fast, but they were in love, and they spent nearly all their free time together anyway.

However, two weeks later, he got fired from his job at the construction site because he was showing up late every day. She made more than enough to pay for the rent on her tiny rental house in the suburbs and the bills even before he moved in, so she wasn't bothered, and he promised he would find a job quickly.

But weeks passed, and all Tony did was stay at home and watch TV or play video games on the couch all day. Her budget was getting stretched thin because she had to pay for food and for dates, but he didn't seem to be picking up on the hints she dropped. The one time she finally worked up the courage to ask him when he was going to find work, he had snapped at her and told her to stop nagging him.

Most people would have recognized things were going downhill from there, but she was blind to it all. Maybe it was because her self-confidence had suffered so much after the fire, or perhaps it was because he turned out to be a gaslighting, abusive asshole.

It was hard to believe she had lived with him for an entire year before she finally saw the light. Well, what she saw was Tony, balls deep inside some random girl in *their* bed after she'd come home early from a shift and found them together.

She gathered up what was left of her confidence and told him it was over and left to stay with her boss. Stacy hooked her up with the job at Rosie's, which she took without hesitation. The next day, Stacy helped her pack up her stuff at her house, making sure Tony was gone, and Temperance put her two suitcases and Fred in her car and drove away.

But it seemed she hadn't learnt her lesson.

*At least things hadn't gone far with Gabriel*, she thought glumly as she pulled the covers up around her. It wasn't even nine o'clock yet she was exhausted. Well, tomorrow was another day—a new day really. There were no limits to starting over, after all, and in the morning, she could begin afresh and this time, she didn't need a pretty boy charmer in her future.

———

One of the great things about working as a baker was that Temperance's body ran like clockwork. She couldn't afford a sleepless night, not when she had to bake dozens and dozens of pies the next day. Though she felt more sluggish than usual today, she managed to get cleaned up and dressed, and out the door by three thirty. After locking the door behind her, she took two steps, then faltered. A strange feeling crept up her spine. Something was *wrong*. Spinning on her heel, she quickly realized why she felt off.

Fred was *gone*.

No, she wasn't imagining it. Only the crown of wilted sunflowers remained in the spot where he usually stood guard. Picking it up, she realized there was a piece of paper underneath.

"What the—"

*Meet me at the pond in Lennox Park at three p.m. or you'll never see Fred again. For each hour you're late, I'm going to chisel off a piece of him and send it to you.*

"That ... bastard!" she exclaimed loudly, crumpling the note in her hands. *He did it.* Gabriel actually kidnapped Fred. "Grrr!"

Stomping to her car, she seriously considered not showing up. They were talking about a plaster and paint garden statue, after all. *I can order another one online.*

But it wouldn't be the same. It wouldn't be the same Fred who drove with her for three days, guarding her belongings at every rest stop and crappy motel along the way, and kept her company through long stretches of highway, and listened to her cry and moan whenever she remembered all the awful things she had endured.

Temperance stewed for most of the morning, burning a batch of pies because she kept thinking of ways to somehow get Fred back without having to see Gabriel. Rosie hadn't been too pissed, but she did have to stay an extra hour to make up for that mistake, and by that time, she only had an hour to get to the park, and she hadn't even had time to eat lunch.

At five minutes before three, she found herself walking up the path toward the pond. It was located in the middle of Lennox Park, and a gazebo sat in the middle connected to land via a wooden bridge. Her heart skipped a beat when she recognized Gabriel's tall frame halfway across the bridge. *Stop it*, she admonished herself. *You're here to get Fred back.*

As she approached him, his eyes went wide. "Temperance—"

"Where's Fred?" she said, cutting him off. "I can't believe you kidnapped him."

"Technically, it's stealing, since he's not a kid," he corrected.

"Whatever," she fumed. "Well, I'm here. Where is he? I want him back."

"I'll give him back," he began. "If we can talk."

"Talk? About what?"

Gabriel paused. "Last night."

"There's nothing to talk about."

"You walked out on our date without an explanation." He folded his arms over his chest. "I know I don't deserve anything from you, but at least tell me what I did wrong so I can apologize properly."

Her chest seized up. She was expecting a fight, a sense of entitlement because he was paying for the date, or even some kind of gaslighting tactic to make it seem like she was imagining things, but not this. Gabriel seemed to surprise her at every turn, and she didn't know what to do. "You didn't do anything," she conceded.

"Then why run away? Because of Vicky? What did she say to you?"

The other woman's name on his lips made jealousy flare up

in her. "Nothing. She didn't have to say anything." Taking a deep breath, she decided that Gabriel at the very least deserved honesty. "We're a terrible match, don't you see? You deserve to be with someone like her. S-someone beautiful and perfect. The way *you're* beautiful and perfect."

"Temperance." His voice darkened as he took another step toward her, crowding her against the railing. "First of all, Vicky may look beautiful on the outside, but she's rotten to the core." He swallowed audibly. "And yes, we were in a relationship, but mostly because our families were, uh, close. Her father and my sister encouraged it, but they only saw one side of her. I, on the other hand, got to see how truly toxic she is. We'd only been dating a few weeks, but she would go on these jealous rages if I even looked at another girl, then make me go through hell to earn her forgiveness.

"Things would be fine after that, and then something would set her off again. It would be some cashier at the supermarket flirting with me or a bartender at a club handing me her number without me asking for it. She would see this and the cycle would begin again—her flying off the handle, me getting down on my knees pleading with her to forgive me. Then one day, I found out the truth—from one of my coworkers actually. Vicky had come to her, and offered her money to come onto me."

"Wait—what?" she asked. "*She* was paying those women?"

His head hung down, then he looked up at her sheepishly. "Yeah. I don't understand it either—I think she got off on seeing me begging for her forgiveness and looking like she was the 'good girl', and I was the playboy she was going to eventually reform. I broke it off with her right then and there." He took a deep breath. "I'm not proud of what I did after—basically slept with a bunch of women, even tracked down those other girls she paid off and slept with them to get back at her. She'd already accused me of having sex with them, so why not? I was spiraling out of control, drinking and sleeping my way through town, mostly to piss off Vicky."

His knuckles turned white as he curled his hands tightly at his sides. "Then Damon came back, messed up from the Special Forces, and he needed my help. I joined the rangers so I could watch over him, even though I hate being outside." He managed a chuckle. "He always said I was the one who saved him from his demons, but I think we kind of saved each other. Who knows what would have happened if I kept going the way I did?"

Her heart lurched thinking of the pain he had gone through, and she stood there speechless for a moment before she found the words she wanted to say. "Why are you telling me this?"

"I'm not really sure." He scratched at his chin. "But, well, I'm not perfect, see? Maybe I was acting crazy because of Vicky, but I was an adult. And what happened after, I'm not proud of it. I was pretty rotten, too, and I regret that I may have hurt people along the way." Carefully, he took another step closer to her. "Maybe you're right, I do deserve to be with her. We're the same, she and I, using people like that."

"Oh, Gabriel, that's not—" She paused for breath. "You don't .... You're not ... I mean, she was a terrible, toxic person and turned you into one too. But you changed, and obviously, she hasn't." It was strange to see this side of Gabriel—vulnerable and raw. "I'm sorry I ran out on you last night without any explanation, that was childish of me. I should have waited for you to explain. I just saw you guys getting so ... close, that I thought maybe you had changed your mind and you would rather have been with her."

"What? Oh no, baby." A hand reached out, landing on her shoulder. "I don't want her. I want you. I like *you*. Is that so hard to believe?"

That voice of doubt in her screamed *yes*. But, looking up

into his sky-blue eyes, seeing raw emotions play on his face, it was hard to believe his words weren't sincere. "I like you too," she whispered. "Can we start again, Gabriel?"

A look of confusion passed across his face before he broke out into a dazzling smile. "Baby, I would love nothing more." His hand crept up from her shoulder to her neck, cupping the left side of her jaw, then he leaned down, his head lowering toward hers.

Oh God, he was going to kiss her!

*Yes!* "Um, can I ask you something first?"

His golden brows knitted together as he stopped halfway. "Okay?"

"Would you really have chiseled parts of Fred off?"

The comment made him laugh. "What? No, I wouldn't do that to poor Fred. And sorry about steal—kidnapping him. I was desperate."

She hadn't thought he would do something as cruel as that. "Okay."

"Okay?"

"Yes. Can you kiss me now?"

"Gladly."

Their lips met in a gentle brush, but it was enough to send a delicious sensation through her body. His mouth moved over hers carefully, but when she let out a low groan, his kisses became more ardent. Hands planted on her waist, his fingers looping into her jeans and tugging her closer until her body was flush against his. God, she could feel how hard and taut his muscles were.

His mouth coaxed hers open, and she complied. His tongue swept inside her mouth, teasing hers until she responded. He tasted like sunshine, all warm and balmy, like laying out on the grass on a summer day. She wanted to experience more of

Gabriel, her mind spinning like a top and making her dizzy at the possibilities.

However, disappointment tugged at her when he pulled away. Did he not like kissing her? "What's wrong?"

He glanced up at the sky and chuckled. "That."

"Huh?" Something wet pelted her on the forehead, followed by another, then another. "Oh!" Their kiss must have short-circuited her brain, because she didn't realize it had started raining.

He grabbed her hand and tugged. "C'mon, let's get outta here."

She followed his lead, doing her best to keep up with him, but his long legs meant that for every step he took, she had to take two. Seeing her struggle, he slowed down. However, the rain quickly turned into a deluge. As the downpour continued, they dashed across the green lawn, giggling and laughing until they reached the parking lot.

Gabriel opened the passenger door of his Jeep, but instead of helping her up to the seat, he scooped her up into his arms. A zing of electricity coursed through her despite the layers of wet clothes they were wearing, though before she could process it, he deposited her into the seat and shut the door.

*Oh. Wow.* And that was just from one touch. How would he feel—

The driver's door opening jolted her out of her thoughts before they turned very R-18. She blushed and turned away from him, hoping he didn't notice her face was red.

"Fuck." Gabriel ran his fingers through his wet locks.

"What's wrong?"

"Fred."

"Fred?" Oh dear, she'd forgotten about her little plaster friend. "Where is he?"

"Back at the gazebo," he said sheepishly. "Sorry. I'll go get him." He kissed her on the lips, then rushed out of the vehicle.

She leaned back on the seat, touching her fingers to her lips. The fluttering in her stomach wouldn't stop—not that she wanted it to. It was still hard to believe—Gabriel liked her. He had gone to all these lengths for her, even bared his worst secrets. He'd kidnapped Fred, for God's sake, so she would hear him out.

A clap of thunder made her look out the window. It didn't seem possible, but the rain came down even harder, and then she saw something coming toward her in the distance. A giggle escaped her throat as the figure came into view—it was Gabriel, running in the rain, Fred clutched in one hand. He dashed toward the car, quickly opening the rear passenger side door. Carefully, he set the gnome in the back before shutting the door. Then, he slid into the driver's seat.

"Sonofa—" He shook his head, sending droplets flying. "Sorry. But I got our man." He cocked his head at Fred, who grinned back at them.

"Thank you for getting him," she said. "I would have forgotten about him." *Because of that kiss,* she added silently.

"Sorry for kidnapping him in the first place," he said sheepishly.

"You're soaked," she said, nodding at his shirt. The white fabric was practically see-through and plastered to his chest. Her throat suddenly felt dry as the desert as her eyes traced the muscles underneath the white fabric. He obviously took care of himself, and while his shoulders and arms were large, they weren't grossly humungous. In fact, he was all sinewy and lean, but underneath his inked skin, there was a power humming that was understated, but unmistakable.

"Temperance?"

His amused tone made her start, and she felt her cheeks

burn. Hopefully he didn't notice her ogling her, but she doubted he'd missed it. *Great.* "You should get dry, before you catch a cold."

His sensuous mouth curved up into a smile and his sky-blue eyes sparkled. "You're right." Starting the engine, he put the Jeep into gear. "I know where we can go."

## Chapter 7

Gabriel couldn't stop smiling after he caught Temperance checking him out. *Yes!* His lion did a little victory dance, swishing its tail. Actually, it hadn't stopped doing that, ever since that kiss. The moment their lips met it was like something in him just knew that this was it: his very last first kiss. There would be no other women for him but Temperance. Her taste, her smell, her feel was imprinted in his brain, and from now until he left this world, nothing would make him forget that moment.

His gamble had paid off. Okay, so it was pretty despicable of him to kidnap Fred. Looking up at the rearview mirror, he stole a quick glance at the gnome through the rearview mirror. He didn't know if it was his imagination, his elevated mood, or that damned thing was magical, but Fred's grin was almost triumphant. *Oh yeah, buddy.* He'd give Fred a little high five later. But for now, he hoped Temperance wouldn't object to their destination.

As they pulled into the garage of the sleek, modern condo building, Temperance let out an audible gulp. "Uh, Gabriel?"

"Yeah?"

"Where are we?"

He parked his car into an empty spot. "We're actually ... at my place."

Hazel eyes went wide as saucers. "Your place?"

"I don't have any spare clothes on me," he said. "And you did say I should get dry before I caught a cold." Okay, so shifters didn't get sick, but he didn't mention that fact to her. "Is it okay if I dry off and change?"

"I guess. But my car—"

"I'll drive you back to the park. You and Fred." He winked at the gnome in the back seat. "Besides, you could catch a cold too. I'll give you one of my shirts, and we can toss your clothes in the dryer." Before she could object, he exited the car and then walked around to help her out.

"Thanks," she said, rubbing at her arms. "I guess I wouldn't mind getting warmed up."

Gabriel could tell, seeing as he could clearly see the outline of her nipples through her shirt. He groaned inwardly, remembering how her tits felt pressed up against him earlier. "Er, it's this way," he said, quickly turning around before she noticed the tenting in his pants.

*Keep it together, Russel.* His main goal for coming here wasn't to get her into his bed, but rather, he just wanted to have her alone and in his den surrounded by his things. He wasn't sure if it was because of their kiss or that he opened himself up to her, telling her things he had never told anyone, but there was a need inside him and his lion to keep her to themselves until that bond formed.

He led her to the elevator, all the way up to his top floor apartment. Since he owned the entire floor, the elevator opened up directly into his living room.

"Wow," she said softly. "This place is huge."

"Er, yeah I got a good price on it," he said sheepishly. It

wasn't that he was ashamed of his wealth, but to him, it wasn't a big deal, really. But he'd grown up with anything and everything he could ask for, and sometimes he forgot that not everyone was as lucky as him. *Thank you, Dad,* he said silently. The small trust Howard had left him had paid for this place and also ensured Gen didn't control all the purse strings.

Temperance already looked apprehensive as she began to soak in the surroundings, probably confused because the mortgage alone on a place like this would cost more than a month's salary for most people. Panic surged in him as she shrank back, and his lion paced, agitated, urging him to do something.

*Do what?*

*Distract her,* it seemed to say.

"Gabriel, how can you afford—"

He did the first thing that came to his head—take his shirt off. Her eyes nearly popped out of her head, and she swallowed audibly. "You should get out of those wet clothes before you catch a cold." Unable to help himself, he looked down to her chest where her nipples were still poking through the fabric.

"What? I—" Glancing down, her eyes widened as she crossed her arms over herself. "Gabriel, why didn't you tell me?"

He grinned. "What do they say? Tit-for—"

"Where's your dryer?" she grumbled as a furious blush crept into her cheeks.

"Hold on, let me get you a shirt first. Sit tight." He bounded to his room, grabbed two dry shirts and towels, then dashed back to the living room. "Here you go. The spare bathroom is the last door there and the dryer is in there."

She murmured a thanks as she slinked away. He breathed a sigh of relief. *Close one.* Temperance would have many questions, and he would do his best to be honest with her. But his family's affairs were the least of his worries. There was another elephant in the room, after all, which was the fact that she was his mate.

It would be difficult to broach the subject with her. When was the right time to do it? His lion was desperate for her to know so they could finish the bonding process. He, on the other hand, knew it was much more complicated than that. Plus, again, there was his family. He couldn't avoid Gen's calls forever.

Growing up, he'd seen as much of his oldest sister as he did his mother, which was to say, hardly ever. After all, she was over ten years his senior and being groomed to take over the company when his mother, Geraldine eventually retired. The plane crash that took his parents' life had been sudden and unexpected, and Gen moving into a leadership position pushed her even farther away from him. As CEO of Lyon Enterprises and Alpha of the Russel Pride, she controlled most of their family holding's business assets. Cool, controlled, and driven, she and Gabriel had often butted heads on many issues, primarily, his role as the sole male of the pride. Gen wanted him to quit the rangers and "take his place" in the company and marry a lioness worthy of his position. But he refused the former, because honestly, dealing with asshole campers and dirt clods in his hair was preferable to sitting in an office from nine-to-five. As for the latter ...

He knew Vicky's sudden resurgence into his life couldn't be a coincidence. Despite the fact that they'd broken up, Gen would always casually mention her and the Woolworth pride or even William, their Alpha and Vicky's father, every chance she could get.

Gen was going to shit a brick when he told her there was no way he was going to marry Vicky or any lioness of her choosing, not when he had already met his mate. Maybe that's why he was desperate to have this mate bond form—then

Temperance would be irrevocably his, and he would belong to her.

"Gabriel?"

He whirled around at the sound of her voice. "Did you find everything okay?"

"Yeah." She padded into the living room in his dress shirt that came down past her knees, rubbing her hair with a towel. Another possessive surge rose in him, and his lion meowed with pleasure seeing her in something they owned. She came closer, but then stopped and quickly turned away when her gaze dropped down to his bare chest.

"Uh ..." Slipping on his shirt, he cocked his head toward the kitchen. "Are you hungry? Did you get a chance to have lunch yet?"

"Uh ..." A growling sound came from her stomach. "Er, sorry. I kind of ... didn't have time to eat lunch."

She didn't need to explain why she hadn't eaten yet as he could have guessed it was because of his ransom note and threat. Guilt poured through him, and his inner lion swiped its claws at him for letting her starve. "I'll take care of that," he said leading her to the kitchen. "Are you famished? I have some chips or fruit you can munch on."

"I'm fine, I can wait," she said as he motioned for her to sit on one of the stools on the center island. "Are you going to order some food?"

He opened the fridge and took out some cheese and apples, as well as a carton of eggs. "No, I can whip you something."

Her eyes went wide with surprise. "You cook?"

"Hey, I'm not *that* much of a bachelor," he said jokingly. "I can cook."

"Oh, no," she shook her head. "It's not that. It's just that ... no one's ever cooked for me before."

"Really? But you're a baker." He pushed the fruit and

cheese at her. "Not even when you were a kid? Like your mom or dad."

A sad look flittered across her face. "Um, not exactly. Unless you count sandwiches and pouring cereal into a bowl." She took the apple and bit into it.

He could tell she didn't want to talk further about it, so he let it be. *For now.* "I'm not a Michelin-star chef or anything, but I've been told I make a mean scrambled eggs. Sit tight."

Gathering the ingredients, he cracked some eggs into a bowl and added some milk and a pinch of salt, then whisked them all together. "Do you want some tea or coffee?" he asked as he turned the stove on to a low heat and added a pat of butter into a pan.

"That would be nice." She put the apple down. "Where's your coffee maker."

"No, no." He waved his hand. "Relax. I'll get it."

He managed to get the coffee started just as the pan was hot enough for the eggs. "I realize I still owe you," he said.

A dark brow rose quizzically. "Owe me?"

"French food and a story," he reminded her. "I said I would tell you why I hate frogs." He poured the eggs into the pan and swirled the yellow creamy curds with a spatula.

She chuckled. "All right, tell me then."

"Well," he began, keeping his eyes on the eggs to make sure he didn't overcook them. "While changing between our animal and human sides is an instinct for shifters, we still need to practice, and so most parents teach their kids how to do it. I was about four or five when I had my first shift. My dad took me out behind our property so I could practice in peace. Unfortunately, my sisters snuck up on us. One of them—I can't remember, but it was probably Gwen—put some frogs in my clothes so that when I put them on, they stuck to me, and I couldn't get them off." As he usually did, he shivered visibly when he thought about that. "I don't remember much of what happened after, only that I was screaming, and my dad came to help me."

"You poor thing," Temperance said. "No wonder you don't like them."

"I know it's irrational, but I really do have all these physical reactions when I see them."

She shook her head. "Not irrational at all. Sometimes, things in our past stick with us, whether we realize it or not. I'm sorry, that was mean of them."

"Thank you." Her concern touched him; the few people he hung out with these days who knew about his phobia still joked about it. "All right, I hope you're hungry."

"That's a lot of eggs," she commented. "You're going to eat some of that, right?"

"Of course."

After he finished plating the eggs, he garnished it with some chopped green onions and pepper. "*Et voilà. Oeufs brouillés, mademoiselle.*" He placed a plate in front of her. "Don't ask me to speak any more French. I'm afraid I nearly failed it back in high school."

"Thank you." She leaned over and took in a whiff. "Oh my God, that smells amazing."

"Why don't you take them over to the couch and we can eat there? It'll be much more comfortable than sitting on these stools." He nodded toward the living area. "I'll get our coffees."

"Thanks," she said, picking up both plates.

After pouring the coffee into two mugs, he joined her on the massive plush sectional couch. "Here you go," he said, handing her one of the mugs, then picked up his plate from the coffee table.

"*Bon appétit,*" she said and then took a forkful of eggs into her mouth. "Oh. Mmmm."

Gabriel swallowed hard as the satisfied sound she made

went straight to his groin. Shifting in his seat uncomfortably, he placed the plate on his lap. As he ate his eggs, he couldn't help but glance over at her, watching as she savored each bite of food he made. It was ironic, really, that he'd been eating her food all these months and enjoying it, and now here she was, consuming something he had made.

They ate in comfortable silence, and once she finished her plate, she put it aside. "Thank you, Gabriel, that was an amazing meal."

His lion was extremely pleased that their mate was fed. "You're welcome." His mouth suddenly went dry as she stretched her legs out in front of her, his eyes tracing a path up her shapely calf, knees, and the creamy skin of her thighs not covered by fabric. *God, I want to be a shirt so bad.*

"I should check on my clothes in the dryer," she said, swinging her legs over the side of the couch. As she got up, however, she let out a sharp yell and fell back. "Oomph!"

Immediately, he sprang into action, catching her in his arms, and they both fell back against the cushion with her sprawling on top of him.

"Sorry, my foot fell asleep," she said. "Um, Gabriel?"

Her sweet scent wrapped around him, and the way her soft body pressed against him sent him into a frenzy. When his erection brushed up against her, she gasped in shock.

"God, woman, I can only control myself so much," he growled. "Let me kiss you again. Please."

She took in a sharp inhale of breath. "Gabriel ... I thought you'd never ask."

*Fuck. Yes.*

He took her mouth hungrily as a possessive streak he'd never felt before swept through him. It was like he wanted to brand her with his lips so she would never forget him. The intensity of his kiss would probably have scared off a lesser woman, but not his mate. No, she responded with equal fervor, mouth devouring his, their tongues dancing and tasting each other.

Her hips ground against his, brushing against his cock with a delicious friction that made him push against her. He needed her so bad, and he could smell her arousal and wetness.

She let out a yelp when he sat up and lifted her so she could straddle his lap. He captured her mouth again, his fingers fumbling for the front of the shirt.

"Gabriel," she squeaked, pushing his hand away. "No."

That single word made him freeze. "I'm sorry," he said quickly. "We don't have to—"

"I can't ... take this off," she said, her lower lip trembling. "Please, I'm not ready for you to see."

*Oh.* He kicked himself mentally. Of course. Her scars. "It's all right ... shh ..." He brushed the single tear that streaked down her cheek. "Don't cry, baby."

"I ... it's not that I don't want to," she said. "I haven't told you ... haven't prepared you. You might change your mind."

Nothing under that shirt was going to make him change his mind, but he respected her boundaries. Someday, she would trust him enough to bare everything. "It's all right. We'll take it slow." Slow for him anyway. She wanted him, though, he could smell it. Feel it in his bones. "Do you want to stop?"

She hesitated. "No ... but, can we keep the shirt on?"

"Whatever you want, baby." His hands moved to her waist, then slipped under the shirt to move up higher, creeping up her rib cage until he reached her breasts. "Yes?"

"Mm-hmm," she hummed, nodding. "You can touch me there."

His hands cupped her breasts, testing their weight. She wore loose, long-sleeved shirts all the time, so he couldn't really tell how large they were, but now, he could feel they were quite generous, a handful even for his palms. "God, your tits feel amazing."

Her eyes blazed as his thumbs found her already-hard nipples. "Gabriel."

"Does that feel good? You like it when I play with your nipples?"

"Yes."

The smell of her arousal became stronger, and she rubbed her hips against him. She seemed to enjoy the dirty talk, which was fucking fantastic because he loved it as well.

Releasing one breast, he slipped his free hand between them, cupping her sex. "Jesus, you're soaked. Is this because of me?"

"Y-yes," she whimpered, rocking herself against him. "Oh. Oh!"

He flicked a finger at her clit, and she cried out. "Please!"

Not wasting another second, he lifted her off him and scrambled to the floor on his knees. Pushing her back, he spread her knees and moved between them.

"Gabriel." Her pupils were blown up with desire. "You can't—"

"I need to taste you, Temperance," he said, hooking one leg over his shoulder. "Will you let me?"

Her plush lips parted, but she nodded.

"Thank fuck," he said before diving in. His hands slipped under her curvy ass, hauling her up to his mouth. She let out a surprised yelp, then moaned when his tongue licked a stripe up her wet lips.

Mother of God, she was delicious. Even better than he'd dreamed. Sweet, with that tang of musk that was all her. He lapped up her cream while teasing her folds, making her pant and moan. Jesus, even her cries were music to his ears.

He slipped a finger inside her slickness, then another, his

cock twitching as she clenched around the digits. He wanted nothing more than to slip inside her and feel that heat and wetness around him, but he had to control himself. He would earn all of her—her trust, more importantly—before he made love to her.

As he continued to lap and tease her with his tongue and fingers, her breath came in shorter pants, and her hips squirmed against him. *Come*, he urged silently as he licked and sucked on her little clit. He wanted to feel her pussy clamp around his fingers when she orgasmed.

"Gabriel!" Fingers shoved into his hair, pulling at his scalp. Her body shook, and her walls tightened and spasmed.

*Fuck!* He looked up at her, watching those plump limps part as she cried out and rode his fingers and lips. He was patient, but he wasn't a saint. Reaching down, he slipped a hand into his pants and wrapped a hand around his cock. It didn't take more than a couple of strokes before his come spurted out all over his fingers as he grunted in pleasure. *Jesus. Mary. Joseph. And all the saints in heaven.* If this was how it was going to be before he even got inside her, he might not survive the real thing.

Temperance whimpered as he slipped his fingers out of her. "Gabriel ... did you ..."

"Er, yeah." Wiping his fingers on his pants, he got up and joined her on the couch, gathering her into his arms and cuddling her to him.

"Should I have ... helped you?" she asked shyly.

He laughed. "Oh no, baby, I wanted you to enjoy the ride." He kissed her hair. "You don't have to do anything you don't want to. This was all about you, baby."

She laid her cheek on his shoulder. "I'm sorry—"

"Stop." He kissed her mouth. "We'll go with your pace, okay? You don't have to do anything you're not ready for. I'll wait." Taking her hand, he kissed her knuckles. "I promise."

"Thank you, Gabriel."

"But, will you stay with me? Tonight?"

She seemed surprised. "You want me ... to spend the night here?"

"Yes, unless you don't want to."

"I do!" She said it so quickly it warmed his insides. "I mean, yes."

"Good. And I mean what I said. I'll be patient. You take the time you need."

Damn it, he would wait for her forever if that's what it took. It would be worth it.

———

While Temperance agreed to spend the night at his place, she reminded him that they both had work early the next day, and he'd also need to take her back to her car which she realized they had left at the park. He said it wasn't a problem as he had shown up to his shift at five anyway, and the timing worked out.

They cuddled on the couch, watched some TV, ordered pizza, and then put on a movie. By nine, Temperance was already fast asleep in his arms, so he took her to his room. She didn't protest or even stir as he slipped her in between the sheets. His chest swelled up with pleasure seeing her there where she belonged—in his bed, in his den. Setting his alarm for three, he cuddled up behind her, nuzzling at her neck and taking in her scent before he fell asleep himself.

He knew his alarm would be going off soon, but he didn't want it to. Didn't want to leave this bed, didn't want to leave Temperance or let her go. She was nestled so perfectly in his arms, their bodies fitting just right. When her hips shifted so her plump ass brushed against his cock, he groaned, feeling it stir. His damned dick reacted immediately, pushing up between her naked cheeks. God, he could smell her slicken, like her body instinctively knew and was readying itself for him. If he was a bastard, it could be so easy to coax her, part her legs and tease her until she begged for it.

But no, he wouldn't do that to her. Not his mate. He would wait—

His lion's ears perked up, and his entire body tensed. The hairs on the back of his neck rose as he heard a noise coming from the living room.

Temperance stirred. "Mmm, Gabriel?"

"Listen to me, okay?" he said in a calm voice. "I want you to stay in here. Do not leave this room under any circumstance."

"What—"

"Stay quiet. I think someone's broken in." His heart thudded in his chest. "My phone's on the nightstand. Get ready to call the police if you hear any screaming or gunshots. Then lock yourself in the closet."

"What? Gabriel—"

"Please. Just do as I say."

She swallowed audibly, but nodded.

Giving her a swift kiss, he rose from the bed, his muscles already tensing. His lion paced, ready to pounce at any moment. Some intruder had dared come into their den while his mate was here? There would be no mercy for this bastard.

Quiet as a cat, he crept out of the bedroom, pressing up against the walls as he followed the sounds of rustling. It was coming from his kitchen, so he crouched low. As a shifter, he could see in the dark so he had that advantage, unless the intruder was a shifter too. It didn't matter anyway, because whoever it was, he'd better be prepared to take on Gabriel's wrath.

His muscles coiled like a spring, then he pounced into the kitchen. "Who the fuck—Ginny?"

"What up, Simba?" she greeted, cocking her head to the side. Dressed in an all-black tracksuit, his sister sat cross-legged on top of the kitchen island.

"What the hell are you doing here?" he groaned.

"What the hell does it look I'm doing?" She nodded at the bowl of cereal in her lap, then spooned a mouthful, crunching noisily.

Gabriel slapped himself on the head mentally. He should have known. His sisters loved messing with him, Ginny especially. "I changed the locks." *Again.*

She swallowed and then hopped off the countertop. "So?" Placing the bowl on the island, she turned around to face him. "How's it going, little bro?"

"You're only ten months older than me, Ginny," he reminded her.

"Which still makes me older. And you the *oops* baby, right?" she said with a maniacal grin, then launched herself into his arms for a hug. "I missed you."

"I missed you too, Gin." He enfolded her in his arms, and they rubbed foreheads together in a sign of affection. "When did you get in?"

"A couple hours ago."

"And from where?"

"Montenegro via Dubai."

Ginny lived a nomadic life, moving from place to place, and never staying more than a few weeks. She claimed it was because she loved to travel and her lioness was restless, but Gabriel knew it was probably because she felt suffocated by living in a small town. He was envious of her freedom on some level, but could understand why she chose to live away: It was difficult to live under the shadows of their sisters.

"How long will you be staying?"

"I'm not sure yet. Actually, I'm here because of you."

"Me?"

"Yeah. I heard some stuff about—"

"Gabriel?" came a voice from behind them. "Where are you? Is everything okay?"

*Shit.* Temperance. Stepping away from Ginny, he padded toward her in the darkness and reached out to grip her arms. "Yeah, it's all good, baby."

She sighed. "I was scared, but then I could hear you talking, what—" A yelp escaped her mouth as the lights suddenly turned on. Her eyes squeezed shut, then fluttered open.

"Oh. Oh, wow," Ginny snorted. "Looks like I was interrupting." Her gaze zeroed in on Temperance. "Hi there."

Temperance tensed. "Gabriel? What's going on? I thought you said someone broke in."

"Someone did," he said wryly. "Turns out it was Ginny. My sister."

"Sister?" One hazel eye widened up at him.

"Ginerva Russel," Ginny introduced. "But you can call me Ginny. And you are?"

"T-Temperance Pettigrew." She remained stiff by his side, unmoving, the right side of her face carefully turned away from his sister.

His sister gave him the side-eye. "Makes sense now."

He was about to ask what she meant, but Ginny gave him a look that said *later*. "Ginny's visiting, from out of town," he explained. "And so, she decided to drop by unexpectedly."

"What Gabriel means is that I like to break into his place for fun," Ginny corrected with a grin. "Sorry for disturbing you, Temperance."

"It's not ... y-you didn't," she stammered. "Gabriel, it's three a.m. I should get ready."

"You go ahead, baby," he said, pressing a kiss to her

forehead. "The spare bathroom should have everything you need. We can leave in half an hour."

"All right."

"It's nice to meet you, Temperance," Ginny called.

"Thanks. Nice to meet you too," she said before disappearing into the hallway.

As soon as he heard the bedroom door close, he stalked to his sister. "Did Gen send you?"

"Did Gen—what the hell are you talking about, Gabriel?" Ginny planted her hands on her hips. "Why would Gen send me?"

"She's been on my case lately," he said. "About—"

"About you doing your family duty?" she finished.

"How did you know if you haven't talked to her?" Gabriel pointed out.

"No, no," Ginny said. "But I've heard some chatter on the grapevine, Gabriel. And it seems like the news is coming from one source: Vicky Woolworth."

"*Vicky?*" he exclaimed. "What has that lunatic been saying?"

"What else?" Ginny grimaced distastefully. She hated Vicky as much as he did, as the other lioness had been jealous of his close relationship with his sister and did everything she could to drive a wedge between them. "Vicky's been insinuating that her father and Gen are this close"—she placed her thumb and forefinger half an inch apart—"to brokering your marriage."

"Fuck that shit!" He slammed his hands on the island counter. "I'd rather have my balls chopped off than be married to her."

"Well, she'd probably do that eventually if you did marry her," she said with a roll of her eyes. "That's why I came back; to warn you and let you know I'm going to disown you if you ever married that cow." She pointed her chin toward the hallway that led to the bedrooms. "And that? What's going on there?" she asked, a brow raised. "I didn't think you were the type to have sleepovers."

"It's not like that." Uneasiness stirred in his stomach, but he knew he wouldn't be able to hide the truth from his sister. "She's mine, Gin."

"Yours?"

"Mine ... my mate."

Ginny gaped. "Your mate?"

"Shhh!" He covered her mouth with his hand. "Temperance doesn't know. She's human."

She ripped his hand away. "And when are you going to tell her?"

"I ..." He blew out a breath. "I don't know how. We only met for real a few days ago. She didn't want anything to do with me at first. I couldn't even get her to come here with me unless I kidnapped her gnome."

"Kidnapped her gnome?"

"I'll explain later," he said. "But you can't tell her."

"Well, you better do it soon," she said. "What are you going to do? About Gen and Vicky, I mean."

A knot twisted in his stomach. "I'll have to figure out what's going on first."

"And shut that lying bitch's mouth," Ginny added.

"Vicky tried to sabotage my first date with Temperance," he said and gave her a quick version of what happened the night at the French restaurant. "And before that, she'd been blowing up my phone with DMs."

"God, what a delusional bitch. What is she thinking? That if she repeated a lie and spread it around enough, it would become the truth?"

"I don't know," he said. "I've been dodging Gen's calls for a while now."

"But—surely she won't make you marry anyone else if Temperance is your mate," Ginny reasoned. "That would be cruel."

"I hope not." But he wouldn't put it past Gen to make his life miserable until he agreed to her wishes. "I'll figure it out, Gin. Listen, I gotta get Temperance to work and then head in for my shift. You need a place to crash while you're in town?"

"Normally I wouldn't say no to an offer from you," she said with a laugh. "But I think you're gonna need your privacy for a couple of days."

"Thanks, Gin." He kissed her on the cheek.

"I'll wait here, and we can ride out together," she said, walking over the sectional and plopping down on it.

Pushing all thoughts of Gen and Vicky from his mind for now, he headed to his bedroom to get ready. When he finished dressing, he swiped his phone from his bedside table, surprised to see that there were already several messages from Anders. "Geez, it's not even four." Opening the messages, he groaned as he read each one.

*So, got that plane ready?*

*We can leave after your shift tonight. Jansen and Grover said they'd cover our shifts for us, but we need to return the favor next month.*

*Cannot wait for Vegas! It's gonna be sick!*

*I'm gonna get so much cat emoji.*

*Hooked us up with some special party favors.* Wink emoji.

The last message was simply the eggplant emoji, water droplet emoji, and peach emoji.

"Fuck me." He had been so busy with Temperance, he forgot about the bachelor party. With the wedding happening next Saturday, this weekend was the only time they would be able to do it, which meant he had a couple of hours to get everything ready and somehow convince Damon to go along with it.

He could tell Anders to pound sand, but Gabriel wasn't the type to back out on an agreement. Now he had to get in gear and plan a bachelor party that the groom didn't want with the time he didn't have.

*This was going to be expensive party.* But it wasn't like he couldn't afford it. If anything, he was more annoyed at the thought of being away from Temperance while their relationship was still developing. His lion, too, was not happy.

*Don't worry, buddy, I'll figure something out,* he said, trying to mollify his animal.

It chuffed at him and tilted its chin upwards in an annoyed gesture, as if saying, *you better*.

## Chapter 8

After finishing her shower in Gabriel's luxurious guest bathroom, Temperance dressed in her freshly laundered clothes from the night before. As she put Gabriel's shirt in the washing machine, she prayed silently that Rosie wouldn't notice that she was wearing the same jeans and shirt from yesterday.

However, while the thought of last night made her go through all kinds of emotions and blush furiously, the one thing she didn't feel was regret. Though they hadn't done anything else after their encounter on the couch, it had been the most intimate she'd been with anyone since Tony. Her ex had been a good lover she supposed, though it was obvious in the waning weeks of their relationship he had been going through the motions. But Gabriel ... he had all his attentions on her, and didn't even ask for anything in return. It was refreshing, but at the same time, she didn't know what to do.

With a deep sigh, she tiptoed out of the guest bedroom. Much to her surprise, Ginny was there, plopped down on the couch, TV remote in hand as she scrolled through the channels on Gabriel's humungous flat-screen TV. Sensing she was there; Gabriel's sister turned her head toward her.

"Hey, come and join me for a bit," she said, waving her over.

Seeing as she had already caught her, Temperance couldn't exactly backtrack to the bedroom and hide out there, despite desperately wanting to. So, she padded over. "Um, hey."

Ginny's gaze was welcoming as she sat, but then it flickered down to her cheek, and Temperance froze, realizing she's forgotten to arrange her hair.

Meeting new people always made Temperance anxious, as they would either gawk at her scars or awkwardly tiptoe around them, pretending they didn't exist. The worst were the pitying looks and those people who simply couldn't stop themselves from asking about how she got them.

"It was a house fire," she explained quickly, wanting to get this over with. "Happened when I was a teenager."

However, when she gazed up into Ginny's blue eyes, there was no pity there, nor did she turn away. There was curiosity of course, but Ginny also looked her straight in the eye with an understanding and acceptance Temperance had never experienced before.

"Oh," she replied. "Gotcha. So, how long have you and Gabriel been—er, dating?"

The question—and Ginny's general demeanor of acceptance of her deformity—had caught her off guard. "Er, we just met. Last night was kind of our … first date. Half date?"

"That's my brother for you. If he can half-ass something, he'll do it. But really, he's a good guy. I hope you'll give him a chance, even if he's not much in the looks department," she guffawed, her eyes rolling.

Temperance laughed at the joke. "Right. I have a really hard time keeping my eyes on him."

"You should put a paper bag on his head. Us Russels are a bunch of hideous hags." Ginny herself was just as good-looking as Gabriel, like a petite, feminized version of him, though her hair was strawberry blonde. "I can tell you one thing: he's loyal through and through. You'll never have to worry about him straying. When he commits to something, he'll finish it."

She bit her lip. It was a little too early to think about commitment, right?

"Did he tell you that he's the youngest of six kids and the only boy?"

"I had no idea." Actually, she realized that aside from not liking frogs and being a lion shifter and a ranger, she didn't know anything about Gabriel.

"Growing up around us couldn't have been easy; hell, I had a hard time myself," she said. "But Gabriel, he took it all in stride. He got teased a lot when he was a kid, but he never once said anything bad about me or my siblings or our family out of loyalty. He's the same with friends and girlfriends." Ginny winced. "Sometimes to an extreme, even if it's unhealthy for him. But family is important to him, and so are the people he loves."

Temperance wasn't sure why Ginny was looking at her funny, but the piercing blue gaze made her shift in her seat. "Uh, okay."

"Are you all done—hey." Gabriel walked into the living room, a blond brow arching at them. "Is Ginny telling you embarrassing stories about me?" he pouted at his sister.

"Like I would tell you if I did." She winked at Temperance, making her giggle.

"No fair," Gabriel said.

As he walked closer to them, Temperance sensed something wasn't quite right with Gabriel. "Is anything the matter? You seem tense."

"Ugh. Yeah." He relayed to them the situation with Anders and the bachelor party.

"Pshaw," Ginny bounded up and waved a hand at him.

"Don't worry, bro. I got a guy who can help. I'll send you his number, and you tell him what you need. He'll take care of everything."

"Thanks, Ginny," he said. "Now I only have to convince Damon to come. He's going to hate it, and he'll be miserable knowing Anna Victoria's at home."

"I have an idea," Temperance blurted out. "Some way you can make them both happy and keep your promise to Anders."

"Really?" he said.

She nodded. "Why don't we head to Rosie's? I can whip up something quick for breakfast, and then we can talk about it there." It would give her time to think about this plan, though she already knew where to begin.

"All right," Gabriel said as he walked to the door and grabbed his keys. "Let's go."

After picking up her car, they drove back to Rosie's, Ginny following them on her motorcycle.

They arrived at Rosie's, and she unlocked the door, letting them in. On the way here, the idea for what she would make the siblings for breakfast was brewing in her head. She told them to get comfortable as she set out to work, going in her usual trancelike state as she got the pies for the day ready, alongside with her inspired original creation. As soon as they were done, she cooled them on the counter, then served it up to Ginny and Gabriel, who were out in the darkened dining room sitting in one of the booths.

"This is ah-maze-balls," Ginny said as she took another bite of the bacon and hash brown pie. "Oh God, marry me, Temperance."

"Hey!" Gabriel protested, then swiped Ginny's plate. "Um, that's your third piece."

She yanked it back. "So? *You've* had four already."

"I'm a growing boy," Gabriel said with a wink at Temperance. "I hope we aren't disturbing you."

"What? No, not at all," she said with a shake of her head. "I don't mind having you both around while I work, and you know Rosie won't fuss over it. Though I do tend to get lost in my own head when I start work, but it gave me time to think." She sat down on the booth to tell them her idea.

"That's actually genius," Ginny said when Temperance finished.

"I don't know why I didn't think of that," he said. "I'll have to hustle to get it all done, but I think it'll work."

"And I'm sure Damon will be grateful," she said.

"Yeah. Speaking of Damon ..." He glanced down at his watch. "I should get to work."

"I'll walk you out," Temperance said.

"Would you mind if I hung around for a bit?" Ginny said. "I'd love to say hi to Rosie. I'm sure she'll be surprised to see me."

"Of course."

She and Gabriel walked out to the back where he was parked. "Now what's wrong?" she asked as they stopped beside his Jeep.

"What?"

"You're frowning again," she said. "Don't you think it'll work?"

"Huh? Oh." He shook his head. "No, it's not that. I just ... I don't want to go to this bachelor party at all."

"Why not? I thought you were the best man? And one of your roles is to plan the bachelor party, right?"

"Yeah, but that would mean I'd have to leave you here for the weekend."

Warmth crept up her cheeks, while butterflies fluttered in

her stomach. "Damon's your best friend. You should be with him and have fun."

"I know," he said, slipping his arms around her. "But I don't want to be away from you." Leaning his head down, he brushed his lips against her forehead. "You should come with us. I'll get us a suite, you can stay there or go to the spa, maybe see some shows."

"Go with you? To Vegas?" She laughed. "You're joking, right?"

"No, I'm serious." The expression on his face told her he wasn't kidding.

"Gabriel, I have to work. Rosie doesn't have anyone else." Oh, she wanted to say yes, there was no doubt. But it was too soon to be going away together. "From what you told me about Damon, it sounds like he deserves all your time and attention this weekend." She gripped his forearms and looked him straight in the eyes. "So go be his friend. Hang out with him while you can, and make this memorable for him. I'll be here when you get back, I promise."

His nose wrinkled. "Fine," he relented. "I mean, you're right about Damon. I'll go to Vegas and get this over with."

An ugly feeling crept into her chest, but she knew she had to say it. "And Gabriel ... it's a bachelor party and everything, and you and I haven't really ... well we only started seeing each other and ..." She took a deep breath. "If anything happens out there, I would understand."

Golden brows knitted together. "What do you—" Sky-blue eyes turned stormy. "Baby, no." He shook his head. "No, no, no." His arms tightened around her. "I won't lie to you because I can guess what kind of 'entertainment' Anders has up his sleeve, but I promise you: there's no way I would be with any other woman but you. Not after last night."

Her heart wanted to leap out of her chest in happiness, but she pushed down the giddy feeling. "But if—"

"No." His voice was more adamant now. "No ifs. No buts."

She let out a squeak as his lips descended on hers forcefully. He pushed her against the side of his Jeep, his body pressing up against hers. A gasp left her mouth as she felt something hard brush against her stomach, and he took the opportunity to snake his tongue into her mouth, tasting and devouring her. She didn't know how long they were entwined like that, but when he finally stepped back, she was boneless and practically hanging onto the side of the Jeep to keep from melting to the floor.

"Remember what I said," he growled.

She nodded, unsure what to do. He kissed her again, softly this time, then moved her aside so he could get into his truck. "Be a good girl now," he said cheekily. "I'll see you soon."

"Uh-huh," she mumbled, her head still reeling from that intense, possessive kiss.

As he drove off, she touched her fingers to her lips, as if she could still feel his mouth on hers. *God, maybe I should have just had sex with him last night.* It was obvious her body wanted him, but she couldn't get over the idea that he would see all her scars. Maybe she could keep her top on or turn the lights off if they did eventually have sex. That's usually what she did in the past. But she had a feeling Gabriel wouldn't be the type to make love in the dark. The thought of him seeing her—all of her—made her anxious as hell, but at the same time, she just wanted to know what it would be like to bare herself to someone without any hesitation.

Turning on her heel, she headed back into the restaurant. Ginny was still sitting at the booth, and when their eyes met, the other woman gave her a knowing look.

"Um, did you need anything else? More coffee?" she asked.

"I'm great, no need to make a fuss." She waved her away. "Go and do what you need to do, I can clean up after us."

"Are you sure?"

"Yeah, I'll be fine. I'll wait until Rosie gets here." Ginny got up and began to gather the plates. "Shoo. I don't want to get you in trouble with the boss."

"All right." With a deep internal sigh, she tried to put that kiss out of her mind and focused on work. It would be a long weekend without him, but soon, Gabriel would be back. Besides, having some space from him might be what she needed to get herself in the right mental state.

———

Gabriel called her a few hours later while she was on her break to let her know he would be gone for most of the weekend. He was successful in convincing Damon to come—as well as put into place the other part of their plan—and would be flying out that evening after his shift.

Disappointment crept into her as they spoke on the phone, but she tried not to let him hear that. Despite his words this morning, the feeling that this was all happening too soon still bothered her. But she went about her day, heading straight home after her shift and went to bed as she usually did. Gabriel had called while she was in the shower, and she called him back right away but he was probably on his flight so didn't pick up. However, she was so tired that she fell asleep before she could even wait for him to call back.

She got up early as usual the next day and saw a missed call from him, followed by a message.

*Sorry we keep missing each other. Anders is being an asshole about cellphone use. Our "package" is being picked up at one today—last chance to join me here.* Smiley face emoji.

Her heart leapt. It was so tempting. But still ...

*Sorry, I can't do that to Rosie,* she texted back. *But why don't you come over as soon as you get back tomorrow? I'll whip up a special pie for you.*

He was probably still sleeping, so she didn't wait for a reply from him, and instead, got ready for work. She went through her morning routine at work as she usually did, though she couldn't help but feel like something was off. Missing even. Oh, it was so tempting to check her phone, but her morning was extra busy, seeing that it was Saturday which meant she had to make more than the usual amount of pies. It was mid-morning, and the dining room was already packed by the time she was able to stop for a quick break and grab her phone.

*Special pie, huh?* Tongue-licking emoji. *I'll be back by six and head straight back to your place. I'll bring my appetite.*

*Oh God.* Heat shot straight to her core as memories of the other night rushed to her brain. Gabriel's mouth on her ... his blue eyes burning like fire as he looked up at her from between her thighs ... that orgasm that shattered her body. *What the hell am I supposed to reply to that?* Maybe something flirty? Or ignore—

"Temperance?" came Rosie's voice as she peeked into the employee's break room.

"Hey, Rosie." Temperance quickly put her phone back into her purse. "Sorry, I was just taking a break." Hopefully Rosie wouldn't notice how red her cheeks were. "I'll get back—"

"It's not that, you know you can take your break when you need to." Her red-painted lips pursed together. "You have a visitor."

"Visitor?" Who the heck would come to her work? She didn't know anyone else in town except Rosie, the employees, and Gabriel.

"Yeah. Says he's from Chicago. Wouldn't give me his name."

Rosie looked annoyed. "Kept pestering Bridgette until she gave in and confirmed you worked here."

*Chicago?* "I'm sorry, Rosie. Let me take care of it."

She followed Rosie to the dining room. Every table was full, so she wasn't sure where her "visitor" was seated, but Rosie cocked her head toward the two-top in the middle of the room. A dark-haired man sat with his back to her, chatting with an uncomfortable-looking Bridgette, who was obviously trying to get away, but at the same time, being polite.

*Oh no.*

She didn't even have to see the man's face to know who it was. If anything, that pit growing in her stomach told her the identity of her visitor. "I'll take care of this, Rosie," she said as she walked stiffly toward him. "What do you want, Tony?"

Her ex turned his head toward her. Slowly, that flirty expression on his face turned into a cruel smile. "Well, look who it is." Whipping back toward Bridgette, he snapped his fingers at her. "Get me another apple pie, will you, sweetheart?"

She ground her teeth together and sent an apologetic look to Bridgette. "He's not staying. You don't have to get him anything," she said, surprised at her own courage. As soon as the young woman was out of earshot, she turned back to Tony. "What are you doing here? How did you find me?" When she left Chicago, she didn't tell anyone where she was going. Only Stacy knew, but she doubted her old boss would have told him. She had hated Tony from the beginning, even before the breakup.

"Baby, you just left without saying goodbye." He mockingly put his hand over his heart. "I was so hurt."

"Really? Didn't that skank I found you in bed with soothe your broken heart?"

"You clearly misunderstood the situation. It's not what you think."

"Not what I think?" He was joking right? She'd seen the evidence with her own eyes. But this was classic Tony. He would deny, deny, deny, and even when there was evidence against him, he would say it was still *her* fault. *God, I was such an idiot.* "I don't have time for this. What do you want, Tony? Is it money? I already paid the landlord the rest of the month, even though I left early. You had plenty of time to move out or sign a new contract."

"Baby, that's not why I came," he said sheepishly. "You just left ... you didn't even give me a second chance."

"Second chance?" she hissed.

"Yeah," he replied. "After everythin' we went through, you just run out like that? Remember when you were sick and I took care of you? Or how about when I took you to that fancy place for your birthday?" He nodded at the obscenely large bouquet of red roses on the chair next to him. "Look, I even got you flowers. Do you have any idea how much these cost me?"

Everything seemed so clear now—all the tactics he used to manipulate her. If only she'd seen it all from the beginning. "Tell me honestly: Was she even the first one? Or just the first one I caught you with?"

Maybe her standing up for herself surprised him, but she saw a flash of guilt on his face, then followed by a sneer. However, he quickly composed himself. "C'mon, baby. You owe me."

"Owe you? I don't owe you anything."

He crossed his arms over his chest and pouted. "Well, I won't leave until you agree to talk to me."

"Excuse me?" Glancing around, she saw the people around them were beginning to stare. "What do you mean?"

"Please, baby." He shot up from the chair, and then got down on one knee. "I love you. I always have, you know that."

His tone was desperate. "What do I have to do to prove it to you?"

She stared down at him, her cheeks growing hot with embarrassment. From across the room, Rosie sent her a disapproving look. "Get up, Tony. *Please.*"

"No." He shook his head. "Not until you agree to talk with me." He swung his arms as if to catch her.

"Tony!" She evaded his grasp by stepping away, but he didn't get up. Staring down at him, she could see the determination—or was that desperation—in his eyes. "Fine," she relented. "Will you leave if I agree to talk?"

He nodded. "Where can we go?"

"I'm working right now, I just can't take off," she exclaimed. Pursing her lips, she continued, "There's a place called Full Moon Diner on Highway Seventy-Five. I'll meet you there at seven thirty." It would be perfect timing so she could tell him she had to go home right away to wake up for work the next day.

Tony shot up to his feet and dusted himself off. "Seven thirty. Don't be late, baby."

Temperance watched him leave, just to make sure he really did go. When the door closed behind him, she let out a sigh of relief. Though a few people were still staring at her, she ignored them, and instead spun around and marched away from the table.

"What do you want me to do about the flowers?" Bridgette asked before she went into the kitchen.

"Ugh, throw them away," she said.

"And, uh," Bridgette glanced around sheepishly. "He didn't pay his check."

Temperance grumbled inwardly. *Typical.* "I'll take care of it. Sorry about that, Bridgette." With a deep sigh, she pushed the door open.

*I should have told him to go fuck off.* That was her thought the rest of the day. Tony was like a disease, and everything he touched turned to shit. Her heart plummeted as her thoughts immediately turned to Gabriel. It was a good thing he wasn't here, because she didn't want to have to explain to him about Tony and the shame she felt at what she allowed him to do to her.

*He can never find out about Tony or that he's even here.* She'd meet Tony and get rid of him before Gabriel came back from Vegas. And for now, she would focus on work and hopefully just get through the day.

The rest of the workday passed much quicker than she wanted, even though she procrastinated and stayed until it was time to leave to meet Tony. She had prepped for tomorrow, telling Rosie she wanted to be ready, but the truth was, there was no way she would be able to stay sane if she went home and waited there for a couple of hours until tonight. Busywork would help her get through the day without anxiety driving her crazy, so she made enough pies to at least get through the next morning. Rosie had asked her if she was okay, but she just waved her away, saying everything was fine.

Soon, she found herself entering the Full Moon Diner at seven thirty on the dot. Tony wasn't there, which wasn't really a surprise. She sat in the farthest booth in the corner, and waved the waitress away when she came to get her order. "I'm waiting for someone," she said. Besides, she wouldn't be able to eat until this entire thing was over and Tony finally got out of town and out of her life.

Tapping her fingertips on the table, she waited. And waited. Finally, it was nearing eight o'clock, and she had just about had enough. Tony always did this, kept her waiting whenever they would meet somewhere, and now she understood that it was his way of keeping her on her toes and asserting his dominance over her, because he knew she would always wait. Knew that she would always feel like she couldn't do better than him and she should bend over backwards to keep him happy. *Well, no more.*

It was strange, but as she got up to leave, a moment of clarity came over her. In the last few months as she'd learned to be independent, be alone and stand on her own two feet, it was now obvious that he'd been the problem all this time. And it was a freeing thought. The inhibitions she felt began to melt away and—damn Tony or anyone else—she was going to get out there and take what it is she wanted, including allowing herself to open up to Gabriel.

Humming to herself as she walked to her car, she was already thinking up a pie recipe to make for tomorrow for Gabriel when she heard someone call her name.

"Temperance! Yo, babe, where are you going?"

Crossing her arms over her chest, she turned around. "I'm leaving. You're late."

"Nah, babe, you're early." Tony held his hands up defensively and shrugged. "You know I'm always thirty minutes late especially since I always get lost in new places. You should have factored that in."

God, Tony was a piece of work. She should just leave him here, but she just wanted this over with. "Say what you need to say, and then you can go."

"Aww, don't be like that, Tempe, baby." He reached out to touch her, but she evaded his grasp. "C'mon now. You didn't even give me a hug and kiss when you saw me."

Was he for real? "That's because we're not together anymore. I would think leaving you should have clued you in."

"Look, you didn't even give me a chance to explain. What happened back home? It's not what you think."

"Oh yeah?" she challenged. "I walked in, and you were naked with her on *our* bed. What were you doing?"

"Just messin' around," he said. "I didn't even put it in that long—"

"Ugh! Stop." She put a hand up. "I don't need to know the details."

"But—"

"But, nothing. The fact is, you're a lying, abusive, gaslighting asshole who's done nothing but made me feel so small that I felt like I wouldn't be able to do better than you. Well, guess what? I've opened my eyes, and I can see what you really are now."

"Babe, I can change," he pleaded. "C'mon, I deserve another chance. Come home with me, please. We can drive away tonight."

"Deserve another ... no." She shook her head. "No second chances. Leave, and never come back." Her foot stamped down in defiance. "I mean it."

Tony froze, as if waiting for her to change her mind. When seconds ticked by and she didn't budge or make a sound, his face suddenly twisted in hate. "I can't accept that, Temperance," he said, eyes narrowing. "I won't."

An unpleasant feeling crept into her stomach. Tony had always been charming and manipulative, using his good looks and sweet words to get his way. However, this man in front of her seemed ... different. Why hadn't she noticed that the hollows of his cheeks were deeper or his hair looked like it hadn't been washed in weeks? His clothes hung off his frame, and was that desperation in his eyes? There was something oddly familiar about the way he looked and acted.

"You need to come back with me, Temperance," he said, advancing toward her. "And you'll do it, one way or another."

She swallowed hard. *Oh God, what the hell was going on?*

## Chapter 9

Gabriel's phone rang constantly all day as he tried to juggle the bachelor party and Damon's "surprise." He couldn't ignore the calls even though they weren't from the one person he desperately wanted to hear from.

His lion sat in the corner and pouted, making its displeasure known at being away from their mate. *Yeah, buddy, me too.* But his best friend was only going to get married once, so he was determined to make this party as successful as possible, even if the guest of honor himself didn't look like he was having fun at all.

Convincing Damon to come had been like pulling teeth, and Gabriel couldn't blame him. However, short of knocking Anders out and then storing him in a shed until after the wedding, there was no stopping the tiger shifter from having this party. Gabriel had to beg, plead, and blackmail the chief, promising him that there would be no shenanigans during the trip.

*At least he didn't seem suspicious that Anna Victoria didn't threaten to leave him when he told her that they were having this party.*

"You owe me, Russel," Damon growled as his eyes narrowed. "You owe me big time."

He sighed. "I know."

"He said we were just going to eat and then go to an early show." The chief's lips pursed as a murderous look passed over his face. "It's five o'clock, and we're at a strip club."

"Hey, there's food here," Gabriel said sheepishly as he nodded at the buffet spread in the corner. "And, uh, there is a stage." God help him, he really wanted to kill Anders.

Gabriel—or rather, Ginny's contact—took care of arranging the jet and the private suite at the ARIA on the Strip, while it was Anders who booked their itinerary. It had been innocuous enough since they started that day—breakfast buffet at the hotel, lounging by the pool all morning, but then the tiger shifter announced he had booked an early dinner and a magic show for them and ushered them into their best clothes.

A stretched Humvee picked them up, and soon, they pulled up to the Pink Palace Gentlemen's Club. Sure, the place looked classy, and Anders—using Gabriel's black credit card—had sprung for the private party room, but Damon would never choose to come to a place like this.

"And that's why I didn't tell ya, because you're all bigger pussies than my tiger," Anders had said as he dragged them inside.

But it was a good thing Gabriel had already guessed what Anders was up to and had come up with a plan that incorporated Temperance's idea.

"Oh yeah, shake it, baby!" a rather enthusiastic voice shouted.

"What the fuck?" Damon's eyes bugged out as he turned his head to find the source. In the center of the room where the small private stage was set up. One of the three dancers had her legs wrapped around the pole and hung upside down as J.D. whooped and showered her with dollar bills.

"God, of course she's enjoying herself," Damon grumbled, rubbing the bridge of his nose with this thumb and forefinger, turning his back from the stage once more.

One of the concessions he had made to Damon was for their other best friend to join, since J.D. was technically part of the wedding party, though she was Anna Victoria's Maid of Honor. Although Anders had initially protested because J.D. was female, the two were now thick as thieves as they ogled and encouraged every single stripper that had performed on stage. Daniel Rogers, on the hand, sat beside them sheepishly eyeing the entertainment, unsure of what to do. He seemed like he wanted to join Gabriel and Damon in the back of the room and ignore the girls, but Anders and J.D. kept egging him on to drop the "nice guy" act.

"Yeah, baby!" J.D. screamed as the stripper worked the pole like she was a Tilt-A-Whirl. "Move that caboose!"

Gabriel stifled a laugh. "Good ol' J.D. doesn't disappoint." He himself glanced at the women disinterestedly. Really, they weren't doing anything for him, and he could tell Damon was just as miserable as he was, being away from their respective mates. Maybe it was time to end this. Pressing the call button in his hand, he waited, and a few seconds later, their cocktail waitress walked in, and he quickly intercepted her by the door.

"What can I get you, sir?"

"How about my special request?" he asked.

The young woman's face lit up. "Ah yes, everything's all set up."

"Good, can you tell the DJ and then let her in?"

"Will do, sir," she nodded. "I'll get you more drinks, too."

"Thanks." *Finally.* He was tired of Damon's brooding, and it would be nice to see him smile.

"What's going on?" Damon said as he walked back to the couch.

"Huh?" he asked innocently.

"Your eye's twitching, and you can barely stop from smiling," Damon pointed out. "Do you have something planned?"

"Hmmm." He plopped down on the couch as the music changed.

"Gabriel—"

"And now we have some special entertainment just for the groom," the DJ announced.

The strippers understood that that was the signal and stopped dancing, then disappeared through the curtains at the rear of the stage.

"Hey!" Anders protested as he waved a fistful of bills. "Where are you going?"

Gabriel caught J.D.'s eyes, who nodded in return. "Anders, c'mon. Let's go to the main room."

"Main room? But we were having fun in here," Anders complained.

Daniel quickly shot to his feet. "Sounds like a plan."

J.D. hooked her arm around the tiger shifter's. "Dude, I think I saw a bachelorette party out there. Bet they're a lot of fun. And looking for some company."

"Really?" Anders's face lit up. "Well then, what are we waiting for? You can be my wing woman, McNamara."

J.D rolled her eyes as she led him out, Daniel right behind them.

As soon as they were out the door, Gabriel grabbed Damon by the arm and dragged him toward the stage.

"Gabriel," Damon asked in a warning voice. "What's going on?"

Now Gabriel didn't bother hiding his grin. "Sit back," he said, pushing him down on the chair. "And enjoy the show."

The lights dimmed, and a slow, sensuous tune began to pipe into the speakers. The curtains behind the stage parted, and a figure wearing a trench coat and a feathered mask walked out in the tallest stiletto heels Gabriel had ever seen.

"What the fuck, Gabriel?" Damon growled. "I told you I don't want any strippers or lap dances or—" He stopped all of a sudden, his entire body tensing.

"Oh, I think you'll like this one," he said with a laugh. Turning his head toward the stage he nodded at the dancer, who whipped off her mask.

"*Jesus Christ,*" Damon cursed.

"Hello there, Chief," Anna Victoria said with a laugh as she sauntered toward them in her sky-high heels. "Surprise!"

Gabriel tossed his head back and laughed aloud. "I guess you won't mind this one, huh, Damon?"

His friend looked up at him, his jaw tensing. "I love you, man, but if you don't get the fuck out of here—"

"I know." He patted Damon on the shoulder as he turned away from the stage. "And there's no one around watching. No cameras, no DJ, no bouncers. You're welcome." He hurried toward the exit, not really wanting to be around for what was to follow.

"Come here, sweetheart," Damon called to Anna Victoria. "How about a lap dance?"

"Nuh-uh, Chief. You can look but you can't—"

Gabriel shut the door behind him, shaking in laughter. *Oh boy, I hope she shows him a good time.* Anna Victoria didn't need a lot of convincing to go along with this plan; in fact, she insisted on it, as with the wedding only a week away, both she and Damon were stressed out and needed to blow off some steam.

As a gift, he'd even booked them a pool suite at The Palms Hotel where Anders would never be able to find them.

*Temperance was a genius, coming up with this plan.*

His lion huffed haughtily, as if saying, *of course she is, she's our mate.*

He sighed and took his phone out of his pocket. Out of respect for Damon, he had put it on silent. He didn't want to be checking on it all the time as this weekend was supposed to be about celebrating his best friend. But Temperance should already be out of work by now, so he could at least give her a call and say goodnight. *Maybe I could convince her to send me some naughty pics.* He groaned as his cock twitched in his pants. Even though he'd been surrounded by gorgeous women all night, only the thought of Temperance made him crave sex.

*Better get outta here or they might get the wrong idea,* he thought as he searched for the door. As he walked toward the exit, he looked back toward the main stage, shaking his head as J.D. and Anders were once again front and center, tossing bills at the stage. Shaking his head, he slipped out the door, breathing in the cool, desert air. Unlocking his phone, he frowned at the ten missed calls and a string of messages from Ginny.

*Pick up.*

*Where the hell are you?*

*You need to call me. Now.*

*It's about Temperance.*

His blood froze in his veins, and his first instinct was to call his mate, but she hadn't called or messaged him. His fingers quickly tapped on the missed calls from Ginny. "What's up, Gin?" he asked his voice tight.

"Oh, Gabriel, thank God! Where the fuck have you been? I've been calling you for ages."

"I was busy," he said. "What's wrong with Temperance?" *And why didn't she call me herself?*

"I'm not sure," she said. "I mean, I went to Rosie's to check up on her, but Rosie said she'd already gone home. But one of the waitresses, Bridgette—she and I go way back—told me about something that happened that morning."

"Something happened?" He already didn't like where this was going.

Ginny sucked in a breath. "Some guy came in looking for her. Brought flowers and everything and caused a scene."

"What guy?" he growled. "Tell me or I'll—"

"Hold yer horses, I'm trying to tell you! So, Bridgette just overheard all this but she says, he got on his knees and wouldn't leave until she agreed to go out to dinner with him tonight at the Full Moon Diner."

"Motherfucker!" His blood was now boiling in his veins. "I'm coming back."

"When?"

"Now." His entire body was shaking with rage, but he somehow managed to hang up the call and then dialed the number for the pilot they'd hired for the weekend. "Get the plane ready, we're headed back to Colorado," he barked at the phone as he waved down a passing cab. "I don't care if you just got back, I want that damned jet ready to take off by the time I get there."

———

The taxi and plane ride seemed like the longest of Gabriel's life. Surprisingly, he looked calm on the outside, despite the turmoil he felt inside. His lion made its wrath known, clawing at him and ripping him to shreds from the inside. It took all his concentration not to shift during the flight, but he didn't want to startle the already distraught pilot. While he didn't want to throw his weight around, this was an emergency, so he was short with the pilot as he ordered him to fly back to Colorado.

Perhaps the worst part of all this was that his imagination had run wild, thinking about all the possible scenarios. Who was this guy? Had she been seeing someone on the side all this time? How could he have missed it? Or was it an old lover? Of course, had his rage not gotten the better of him, he could have called her for an explanation, but he was already in the air by the time he thought of that.

*It didn't matter*. Temperance was *his*, and he would fight for her with literal tooth and claw if he had to. There was no outcome in this scenario where he would not be the victor, and by the end of the night, she would know who she belonged to.

The door to the plane barely opened before he rushed out, taking the stairs two at a time and ran all the way to the parking lot of the private airstrip in Verona Mills where they landed. It was already past seven, and it would be another hour drive to that diner Ginny had told him about. He floored it and his Jeep ripped into the parking lot around eight o'clock. He didn't bother to park his car, because his vision turned red as soon as he saw his target.

Temperance was by her car, while a man stood over her. He advanced toward her and grabbed her arm, making her jerk back. Fury burned through Gabriel as he slammed on the brakes and flew out the door. His lion roared in outrage and pressed its claws at his skin, wanting to get out. He was sorely tempted to give in to his animal, but this was not how he wanted to introduce his lion to their mate.

"Get the *fuck* away from her," he roared.

"Gabriel!" Fear, and then relief spread across Temperance's pretty face as she wrenched free of the man's grip and then cowered back, pressing herself up against the side of her car.

The man who attacked her turned around; his face twisted

in rage. "Who the hell are you to tell me what to do?" As if to make a point, he began to inch toward Temperance.

Gabriel rushed toward them, stretching out to full height as he focused on the other male. "I said, get the fuck away from her." Opening his mouth, he bared his sharp teeth as his canines grew to full length, then let out an inhuman roar, making the man jump back.

"Jesus H. Christ!" he exclaimed. "You're one of *them*."

"You bet your skinny ass." He stalked toward Temperance, placing himself between her and the other man. Her face was ashen, and she seemed frozen. "Are you okay, baby?" he asked, his voice turning gentle.

"Are you fucking this ... this freak, Temperance?" the guy suddenly screamed.

Temperance flinched. "That's none of your business, Tony," she squeaked.

"Oh, it is my Goddamned business," Tony yelled back. "I'm your boyfriend and—"

Gabriel spun around. "What?"

"*E-ex*-boyfriend," Temperance qualified. "I left, remember?"

"But you didn't give me a chance to explain." Tony stepped forward, but Gabriel continued to block him, arms crossing over his chest. "Please, Tempe babe—"

"Stop calling her that," Gabriel hissed. "Actually, just *stop*. Stop talking to her, stop looking at her, and stop thinking about her. She obviously left your ass for good reason and doesn't want to see you anymore."

Tony's nostrils flared. "Listen here, you dumb fuck. You know nothing about Temperance and me—"

"There is no Temperance and you," Gabriel interrupted.

"She doesn't know what she wants," Tony said. "Right,

baby? You're always changing your mind. I know what's good for you. Just listen to me and stop being stubborn."

There was a desperation in the other man's voice that set off alarm bells in Gabriel's head, but for now, all he wanted was for this asshole to get out of his sight. "Seems to me she knows exactly what she wants, or rather, doesn't want: You. Moving across the country is a pretty clear signal."

Tony bristled. "Why don't you take a hike? Just because you got into her panties once doesn't mean you get a say in what she does. What she really wants—and needs—is me."

Gabriel tamped down the urge to kill him on the spot. "Tony, is it? I know your type—you like to talk big, probably compensating for ..." His gaze dropped down to his crotch. "Something else. But what you really are is a big bully."

"Oh, so you know me, huh?"

Oh, he knew Tony's type all right, and it all made sense why Temperance seemed shy and withdrawn. He wouldn't be surprised if this Tony guy was the reason she couldn't believe Gabriel—or anyone—could possibly love her for who she was.

"Looks to me like she's seen the light. Let me guess, you cheated on her multiple times? Trying to make yourself seem like the big macho man, having a nice girl like her at home doing your bidding while you go out and wiggle your shrimp dick at anyone who even gave you a second glance—"

"Fuck you, freak," Tony snapped. "She was mine first —ack!"

The human didn't manage to finish that sentence, not with Gabriel's hands squeezing his neck tight. "Listen here, maggot." He slammed Tony's body up against the car behind him. "She was yours first? Then you should have done everything in your Goddamned power—even sold your soul to the Devil himself— to keep her." His lion urged him on, their claws extending out from his fingers just enough to prick at the other man's skin.

"That's what I would have done. But she's mine now, and if you even think about her or breathe the air she does, I'm going to open you up from neck to balls and eat you alive, got it?"

Tony took a gulp of air when Gabriel loosened his grip, and managed a nod.

"Christ." The smell of urine made Gabriel want to gag, so he let go of the other man. "Get the fuck out of here."

As he scrambled to his feet, Tony sent him a death glare. "You two freaks deserve each other," he spat as he stomped off toward the rusted-out sedan near the front of the parking lot.

Gabriel took a few deep breaths and counted to three, watching as Tony peeled out onto the highway. Slowly, he turned around. "Baby, are you—Temperance?"

He expected her to still be plastered against the side of her car, but instead, she had rounded to the driver's side, tugging at the handle desperately in an attempt to open the door. Her movements were manic, and her entire body shook as she let out a shriek of frustration when the door remained shut.

Patiently, he walked around to her side. "Maybe it would help if you unlocked the door first?"

She whirled around; light hazel eyes wide, cheeks flushed red.

"Where are your keys, baby?" he asked.

Her lips parted, and she sucked in a breath. "I-in my p-purse." Her bottom lip trembled, and her eyes glistened with unshed tears.

Gabriel's chest tightened. "Baby, I'm so sorry for—"

"He's right," she whispered, a single hot tear streaking down her cheek. "I am a freak. You shouldn't—"

"No, no, no." More tears poured down her cheeks. "Oh, baby, please don't cry. You don't know what it does to me."

Slowly, he approached her, arms reaching out. Though she flinched when his hands touched her shoulder, he embraced her anyway. She didn't struggle, but instead, burrowed her face into his chest.

"You're not a freak, baby. And that asshole doesn't know what he's talking about." He tightened his arms around her. "He called me a freak, too. And you know what? I don't give a shit what he thinks. If it means I do deserve you, then I'd gladly call myself a freak."

She looked up at him. "You know you're not. And that's not what I meant." Disentangling herself from him, she nodded down at her right arm. "You shouldn't be with someone like me. I don't deserve—"

"You know I don't care about that."

"What you can see now? It's nothing compared to the rest of me." She began unrolling her sleeve, exposing the frightening sight of the patches of discolored skin and webbed tissue on her arm. "It goes all the way up, to my back and neck. I'm mostly bald under here, too," she said, shoving her fingers under her neck. "What is everyone going to say when they see us together? Oh, I know." Her lips thinned. "They'll always wonder what someone like you is doing with someone like me. That's what they would always whisper when I was with Tony. And I couldn't keep him, and I certainly won't be able to keep you."

"Stop saying that!" That made her jump back, and he cursed softly. "Maybe he wasn't worth keeping." A thought popped into his head, and it made him want to murder the other man even more than he already did. "Did he ... was he the one responsible for your scars?" If she said yes, God help him, he would hunt that bastard down right now.

"What?" She double-blinked. "No, no, he wasn't." Her shoulders sank, and she sighed. "I was sixteen when it happened. My m-mother and stepfather, they weren't ... good people. I mean, they never hit me or anything, but all they cared about was getting their next hit. They'd been addicts since I could remember." The light in her hazel eyes seemed to die, as if she was trapped in some nightmare in her mind and couldn't get out. "We moved into a motel because we'd been kicked out of our last apartment again, and I had to sleep on the rollaway bed. I went to sleep early because it was exam week. The next thing I knew, I was in bed and everything was hot. I couldn't breathe. And the burning ... I passed out and woke up in the hospital. I was the only one that survived."

*Oh God.* Gabriel's chest was constricted so tight he couldn't breathe. "Temperance ... that's horrible. I'm sorry."

She shrugged. "It's been a long time. I mostly got over it. Had the surgeries, therapy, learned to support myself ...." Her nostrils flared. "Then I met Tony. He was ... everything you could want in a boyfriend. He paid attention to me, took me out. He was so out of my league."

He snorted as ugly jealously crept into his gut but let her continue.

"He moved in right away, then he changed. Lost his job, and I had to support him." Her expression darkened. "When I complained, he was always reminding me how I couldn't do any better than him and how no one would ever love me because of my scars. When I cried because I was so hurt, he would tell me he didn't say those things or say they were just a joke. He also cut me off from my friends, saying that they were all jealous of me whenever they tried to tell me he was controlling. It took me catching him in bed with someone else to finally get the courage to leave him."

"I'm glad you did," he huffed. "He was a terrible person, a predator of the worst kind." His fingers curled into his palms. "He saw you as vulnerable, your self-confidence barely holding together and knew he could take advantage of that. I'm sorry he did that to you, but I'm not sorry he drove you out here so we could finally meet."

"Why do you keep saying stuff like that?" she cried.

"Stuff like what? That I'm glad I finally found you?"

"Like that!" She gritted her teeth. "Sweet, amazingly kind things that make me ... make me want to ..."

"Make you want to what?"

"Make me want to hope," she choked out. "Hope that I could possibly hang on to you and keep you."

"What?" Genuine shock made his jaw drop. "Baby, you *are* keeping me. And I'm keeping you." Unable to help himself, he trapped her in his arms. "Temperance, look at me. Please." Slowly, she lifted her head to meet his gaze. "You said you liked me too, right?"

She nodded.

"Do you feel this ... connection to me? Anytime you see me, even from a distance, something in you just can't look away, and you want to be near me? Or when we're far apart—like last night —you just can't sit still, and all you can think about is me."

Her eyes went wide with wonder, though she didn't say anything. She didn't have to. Hope soared in his chest. "I know this is going to sound crazy ... but Temperance, you're my mate." He hadn't planned on telling her this way, but it seemed like the right time. "*My* soulmate. Us shifters, we have this one person that we're supposed to be with and while our human selves may not see it right away, our animals always do. Hell, my lion must have known even before I crashed into the kitchen, because I kept coming back just for your cooking."

"I don't understand, Gabriel," she began. "We're soulmates?"

"Search inside yourself, Temperance. You know it's true."

As her lashes lowered, a sense of dread crept into his stomach. Temperance was human. She had no animal to tell her this. What if she couldn't understand? Or what if she rejected him anyway?

Seconds ticked by, and finally clear, light hazel orbs looked up at him. "Somehow, I always knew. Whenever I was baking, I would always think if you would like this kind of ingredient or that ... and when you came in, I would always watch you through the window in the kitchen. I would feel so happy when you ate every single one of my pies. And it wasn't just because you were good looking." She smiled sheepishly. "Is that silly? Or—"

"Not at all," he said. "You're my mate, Temperance. And I'm yours."

"Gabriel," she sighed. "I was so afraid if you found out Tony was here ..." She swallowed audibly. "That you'd think I asked him back. And that I wanted him here. But I didn't. I don't."

"What? Oh no ... baby." He held her tighter. "I would never think that. I told you, you're my mate. Nothing you could do or say could make me think otherwise." As he lowered his head, his heart drummed against his ribcage.

She opened up to him eagerly, leaning back as their mouths touched. Pure joy burst through him as they kissed, his lips moving over hers in an ardent caress. A gasped escaped her mouth as he delved his tongue into her mouth, tasting her sweetness. His entire body vibrated with need, and he pulled away. "Temperance. Come home with me tonight."

Her pupils were blown with desire. "Yes," she said in a husky voice that made his cock immediately harden.

Somehow, they both found their way to his Jeep. The engine was still running, which made it easier to maneuver out of the parking lot and into the highway. It was a miracle they didn't get into an accident as his mind was on Temperance and taking her—all of her, finally. He kept biting the inside of his lip as he drove home, as he pulled into his parking spot and then led the way up to his condo. As soon as the door closed behind them, he turned around and caged her in his arms. "Temperance ... I want you so bad."

"No more talking," she urged, nipping at his lips. "Please, Gabriel."

Damn, his mate had bite. Bending down, he swooped her into his arms, fearing that if he even kissed her he would take her against the door. No, their first time would be in his bed, and he would make sure she would never forget it.

He carried her all the way to his room, laying her down on the bed gently. "Temperance, will you let me see you? Please?"

"I'm scared, Gabriel," she said in a small voice.

"There's nothing to be scared of," he said, pressing soft kisses down the right side of her face. "I promise."

She sucked in a breath, and then he felt her nod. Joining her on the bed, he positioned her so she was leaning back on his headboard and he knelt between her knees.

Crawling back, he started with her shoes, slipping them off and tossed them off the side of the bed. His fingers traced up her bare legs, over the skirt covering her hips and thighs until he reached the waistband and pulled that off too. The tiny lacy panties she wore covered up what he had already seen and tasted the other night, but damn if it didn't make him harder, seeing the shadow of her dark pubic hair through the white fabric and the smell of her wetness teasing him. Though he wanted nothing more than to take her, he knew he had to be patient.

"Do you want me to—"

"May I?" He crawled back up, reaching for the front of her blouse. Slowly, he undid the buttons, one by one, baring her lace-covered breasts. He'd been dreaming about those sexy tits for two nights now, wondering how they would feel and taste. But again, he had to help Temperance get over her fear of being naked around him. So, he slipped the top off her shoulders, easing it down her arms, all the while keeping his eyes on hers. He could see the anxiety growing in those light hazel orbs. "Don't be scared," he said as he helped her remove her left arm from the sleeve. "There's nothing to be worried about."

Her lower lip trembled. "I can't help it."

"Trust me, Temperance. I'm your mate. You're the other half of my soul. This body, in whatever shape or form, was made for me. Has always been." He took her right hand, the sleeve still hanging off it and covering her to her wrist, and kissed the webbed skin behind her palm and nuzzled it. "You're beautiful to me, no matter what."

He heard the sharp intake of breath, and she sat up, tugging the shirt off. He held her hand so that she wouldn't cover herself, then finally looked up at her, bared before him.

The scars did indeed cover her from fingers to cheek, a patchwork of discolored skin and latticework of puckered flesh. He took in the entire sight before him, then looked her straight in the eye. "See? That wasn't so bad, was it?"

She shook her head. "But ... my scars ..."

"I'm not going to lie to you and pretend they're not there or even give you trite or cliched expressions you've probably heard before," he said. "But I want you to know, those scars have nothing to do with who you are as a person now."

"And who am I, Gabriel?" she asked, her voice quavering.

"You're Temperance Pettigrew, a talented and beautiful woman. You frustrate me sometimes, but you always make me laugh. You're loyal and kind to a fault, but you would do anything for your friends, even if they were made of plaster." When she snorted, he pounced on her, covering her body with his. "You challenge me and make me want to be a better person." Lowering his head, he whispered in her ear. "And you're mine, and I want *you*."

# Chapter 10

*You're mine and I want you.*

Those words, and Gabriel's breath hot on her skin made Temperance shiver. But it was the truth behind them, the veracity she knew deep in her bones that made all her doubts fall away.

"Gabriel ... I need you ..."

The soft, needy growl from his lips made desire shoot straight to her core, making her slick in anticipation. His mouth devoured hers hungrily, eagerly, and she let him in, allowing his tongue to taste and taunt her at the same time, his masculine flavor dissolving on her tongue like herbed butter on steak. She wanted more—she wanted all of him.

Pushing him off her, she reached down and grabbed the hem of his shirt, pulling it all the way up and over his chest. He helped her whip it off and toss it aside, then trained those sky-blue eyes on her.

God, he was beautiful. Reaching out, she traced the muscles on his shoulder with her fingers, feeling the hard muscle under his hot, tanned skin. She trailed her mouth alongside her hands, kissing every inch of him. His collarbones, the dip under his throat, the line between his pecs. When she reached the hard-tipped flat nipple, he let out a groan when she flicked her tongue out to tease him.

With a growl, he flipped her onto her back, making her squeak. "You're mine now," he said, grinning at her. Pinning her hands to her sides, he lowered his head, giving her a quick peck on the mouth before he went straight for her cleavage. His tongue traced the line between her breasts, burrowing deep into the flesh, tickling and teasing her until she was moaning and squirming under him.

"Gabriel," she exclaimed when he tore the lace that held her bra cups apart, her breasts bouncing to freedom. Immediately, he claimed one nipple with his mouth, tongue lashing and lips sucking back. The sensations made her roll her eyes back in pleasure and rake her fingers into his hair to pull him closer.

She moaned in disappointment when he pulled away. Looking down, she saw him trailing kisses lower ... "Oh!" His mouth was on her again, fervently licking and sucking at her slick pussy lips. Tongue, mouth, teeth worked at teasing her relentlessly until she had no choice but to be swept away in orgasm.

He didn't stop at one orgasm or even two. Gabriel seemed to be determined to wring every ounce of pleasure he could from her, licking and sucking at her, teasing her clit and thrusting that talented tongue of his as deep as he could inside her. It only took a couple of hard thrusts before she was coming again, her hips lifting off the bed to meet his mouth, the growling and snarling in his throat pushing her over the edge.

"Gabriel ... I need you so bad," she panted. "Please."

He grunted as he pushed away, fumbling at his jeans as he shoved it and his briefs down, his thick cock springing free. Her pussy practically throbbed seeing how large he was. Spreading her knees wide, he covered her body, his cock pressing against her belly, teasing her. "Gabriel ..."

"Easy, baby," he whispered. "You'll get what you want. But first ..." His arm reached out to the side of the bed and pulled a silver packet out of the drawer.

"Oh, thank goodness." She wouldn't have thought of that. While she knew she wanted children, she wasn't quite ready yet. Even if the thought of having Gabriel's baby did make her feel giddy.

Quickly, he ripped open the package and slipped it over his shaft. The blunt tip nudged at her core, and Gabriel grit his teeth as he pushed in slowly.

"Temperance ... so good," he groaned when he was finally fully seated in her. "God ..."

"You too."

Gabriel pulled back, slowly and surely, then slammed back inside. There was no time to be surprised as his smooth movements began to even out, bucking into her in a steady pace that had pressure building up inside her. "Gabriel!" She arched her body up, begging for more, needing more from him.

His pace was punishing, relentless as he continued to rut into her until she was squeezing around him, her orgasm ripping through her like a lightning strike. All of a sudden, she found herself on top, straddling him, Gabriel grinning up at her. "You're so beautiful, my mate."

She gasped as he thrust up at her, his cock hitting a different part of her that made her shiver. Bracing herself on his chest, she began to move, rocking her hips back and forth, feeling her clit rub against his pubic bone in a delicious way.

"That's it, baby," he encouraged. "Do it. Make yourself come on my cock."

"Gah!" Throwing her head back, she increased her pace. It was incredible, this feeling, looking down and watching his face twist in pleasure, knowing she was the cause of it. It made her move faster, gyrating her hips until he was biting his lip.

"Temperance, I—" He groaned as he grabbed at her hips, ramming her down as his pelvis piston up into her. "Fuck, I'm coming!" His eyes closed, head slamming back on the pillow as she felt his cock pulse with his orgasm. She raked her fingers down his chest as her own pleasure washed over her like a wave, making her body shudder over and over again until she felt drained.

"Oh, Gabriel," she said in a breathless voice as she collapsed against him. "That was ..."

"Phenomenal," he finished. "Mind-blowing. Let's do it again."

She giggled when he rolled her over. "Again?"

"Mm-hmm." He licked at her neck, making her moan against him. "Do you need to get up early?" he asked. "To get to work?"

"I stayed and ... oh, Gabriel ... did some prep work," she panted. "I can be an hour or two late."

"Good. I don't need much sleep, but I can let you crash for a couple of hours."

She could feel his cock getting hard again. "Then you'll be done with me?" she teased, running her nails down his back.

"Oh no, baby," he murmured against her skin. "I'll never be done."

———

For the first time ever in her life, Temperance was late to work, much later than she'd anticipated, actually. It was nearly eight o'clock by the time she arrived at Rosie's, but much to her surprise, the kitchen was already humming with activity, and the smell of fresh pastry filled the air.

"I'm so sorry," she said to Rosie, who was taking a pie out of the oven. "I was, uh, delayed."

"I had a feeling you might be late," Rosie's lips curled into a smile.

"You did?"

She cocked her head behind her, where Ginny was sitting on top of the counter, digging into a slice of apple pie with a fork. "Hey, Temperance," she greeted after swallowing a mouthful. "Glad to see you're okay."

Gabriel had explained why he came back from Vegas and how he had heard about Tony harassing her. "Oh, hey, Ginny."

"Well, it's a good thing you did all that prep work," Rosie said. "All I had to do was put everything in the oven. Did you have a good evening?"

Temperance felt her blush from head to toe. "It was nice."

"Just nice?"

"I—"

The door crashed open behind her as Gabriel rushed in. "Jesus, babe, I'm so sorry I made you late. Don't worry, I'll charm—Rosie," he greeted the fox shifter with a sheepish grin. "Good morning."

She returned it with a knowing smile of her own. "Gabriel. Do you want some breakfast?"

"Uh, yeah. We didn't have time to eat before coming here."

"I'm sure you didn't," she said with a chuckle. "Go ahead and help yourself." She nodded her chin at the half-eaten pie next to Ginny. "You too, Temperance. You have some time. Sit and eat up. I'm sure you'll need the energy."

She glared at Gabriel and whispered, "I told you we didn't have time for that quickie."

"Hey, I never said it would be a quickie." He wiggled his eyebrows at her. "C'mon, I'm starving."

As they grabbed some plates, Temperance couldn't help but

ALICIA MONTGOMERY

wonder if Rosie and Ginny knew about her and Gabriel being mates. They probably did. Part of her was self-conscious about it, but at the same time, she found herself not minding.

Gabriel's confession to her had been a shock, but somehow, she'd always known. She may not be a shifter, but something inside her told her that it was true. It was hard to describe that feeling, but it was something akin to her gut instinct about baking and which ingredients would go well together. Somehow, despite not making sense, she and Gabriel just worked.

After she finished eating, she shooed Rosie off into the dining room because it was starting to fill up. Weekends were their busiest time, so she knew she had to get to work as they would soon run out of pies. As she worked, the Russel siblings stayed but mostly kept out of her way. When she took short breaks, she found herself chatting with Ginny.

Gabriel's sister was no-nonsense and blunt, and while her personality type would normally have repelled Temperance, she couldn't help but like her. Plus, she loved hearing about Ginny's travel stories, whether it was hiking to Petra in Jordan or scuba diving in the Maldives. She also grilled Ginny about her favorite foods, and hearing her describe things like the sweet and savory *knafeh* from Turkey or sticky mango rice from Thailand were already getting her creative juices flowing with ideas for her next recipes.

When she was done for the day, Gabriel coaxed her into going back to his place, though she did make him drive her to the Full Moon Diner to get her car and go back to her place to get a change of clothes. They went back to his condo where Gabriel made them dinner again and then spent the rest of the night making love in his bed.

Temperance had never been the type to crave sex, but with Gabriel, it was like she couldn't get enough. Plus, he was an amazing lover. Attentive, playful, and considerate, but also dominant in a way that made her want to submit to him. It was almost disappointing to have to leave again for work the next day, but they both had responsibilities.

"Did you get a chance to talk to Damon?" she asked as he walked her to the kitchen door at Rosie's.

"Yeah, yesterday while you were working," he said. "Don't worry, he's cool with me disappearing. He says he understands, plus, he was too busy with Anna Victoria anyway," he added with a chuckle.

"Good." She felt terrible that Gabriel had had to leave the party so abruptly. "I'll see you after work?"

"Mm-hmm." He pushed her up against the door. "I'll miss you until then." Before she could protest, he kissed her thoroughly, leaving her breathless. "I'll see you later at the French place at six?"

She stared after him, waiting for him to drive off before she went inside. *Time to get to work.* As she prepped for her day, she wondered if she had ever been this happy before. Maybe, but she couldn't remember. Or all those other times were eclipsed by what she was feeling right now.

By the time Rosie came in, she was humming to herself, thinking of tonight when she would see Gabriel again. Rosie flashed her a knowing smile but said nothing and mostly left her alone. Even though she was done at one o'clock, she stayed and worked on her new recipes for the rest of the afternoon, not really wanting to wait in her empty trailer until it was time to meet Gabriel. When she was finished at five, she said goodbye to Rosie and Bridgette and walked out to the parking lot feeling like she was floating on air as she made her way to her car.

"Well now, don't you look so full of yourself?"

She froze midway as she was reaching for her car door. Slowly, she turned around.

Vicky Woolworth stood behind her; arms crossed over her ample chest displayed in a beautiful low-cut designer dress. However, her perfect outfit, hair, and makeup couldn't hide the ugly sneer on her face.

"Can I help you?" Temperance asked in a calm voice.

"Sure, you can." Vicky smile didn't quite reach her eyes. "By leaving me and Gabe alone."

"Excuse me?" Her arms stiffened at her sides. God, she hated this woman for what she did to Gabriel.

"You poor, pathetic little human," she cooed. "You really don't know who you're dealing with, do you? The Russel's lineage has been untainted for generations, and they certainly won't be allowing someone like you to muddy their bloodline. Not when they have prime Woolworth stock available."

*What was she talking about?*

"Oh." Vicky covered her mouth as she laughed. "I guess you really have no idea."

"No idea about what?" God, she wished her voice didn't tremble.

"What's been in the works for a while now." Her stiletto heels clicked on the asphalt as she took a step forward. "Gabriel and I are engaged to be married."

Her blood froze in her veins, and her heart stopped for a second. "*Engaged?*"

"Yes," Vicky said. "Sure, we broke up for a while, but it was only because we were both so young. I understand that he needed to get that energy out of his system—sow his wild oats and whatnot—but now it's time, and our families have come to an agreement." She bared her teeth, glossy red lips parting. "So, I suggest you get out of the way, or *else.*"

Temperance stared at the other woman, the seconds ticking by. Then that voice in her head came back.

*Of course he's engaged.*

*Vicky is who he deserves to be with. Perfect and beautiful. Gabriel will never want you.*

A pit began to form in her stomach. *No!* she screamed at her inner voice. *You can't control me anymore! Gabriel is my mate!*

A lightness, a kind of clarity washed over her. Then, she began to chuckle. Soon it became a full, lengthy, cackling laugh that had her clutching her sides. "M-m-married?" She managed to choke out between giggles. "Oh my God, you're so pathetic."

"What—what are you doing? Are you making fun of me?" Vicky screeched, her eyes flashing. "No one makes fun of Vicky Woolworth! Stop it, stop it right now!" She emphasized her orders by stamping her feet.

"Oh God ..." She wiped the tears from the corner of her eyes. "Listen, you delusional cow," she began as she managed to get ahold of herself. "Gabriel *hates* you. You had your chance, but you blew it because you're vain and insecure, wanting him to prove his love to you all the time. And now he'll never want you again, and that's all your fault."

Vicky's face turned an alarming shade of purple. "You *bitch!* You should have left and gone back to Chicago when you had the—"

"*Vicky,*" came a deadly voice from behind. "I suggest you choose your words carefully. Or not say anything at all."

The lioness's face crumpled, and she slowly spun on her heel. "Gabe! Thank God you're here!" She sauntered over to him, arms reaching out, but stopped when he sent her a warning glare. "Your ... your human was threatening me!"

Gabriel's eyes blazed as he folded his arms over his chest. "That's not what I heard. Sounds like she was giving you a pill that's hard to swallow."

Her shoulders stiffened. "You can't mean to choose this ... this insignificant little human over me? Our families have been friends for years. What would Genevieve say?"

"First of all, Gen has nothing to do with this," he said. "And second, I'd love to hear her thoughts when she finds out you've been spreading rumors about our supposed engagement."

"It was just a matter of time—"

"Well, it's the first I heard of it. You know that's not how it works," Gabriel said in a warning tone. "And if you think spreading your lies will get you what you want, then perhaps you don't know Gen at all. She doesn't like being told what to do."

Vicky swallowed audibly. "You'll pay for this, Gabriel Russel." Her nostrils flared as she fisted her hands at her sides. "You and your stupid little human slut!"

"Vicky," Gabriel roared.

"You had your chance," she told Temperance. "Now you'll regret not taking it."

"Leave," Gabriel ordered. "Now, or I swear to God—"

"Fine," she harrumphed, then turned around, marching all the way back to the bright red BMW a few feet away.

As Vicky's car roared out of the lot, Gabriel rushed to her side. "Temperance, are you okay? What else did she say to you?" He raked his hands through his hair. "Oh God, I'm sorry. I should have told you ... I just didn't know how. Please, baby," he begged. "Forgive me."

"Forgive you?" she asked. "For what? She was the one who was lying."

"Uh ..." Gabriel took a deep breath. "It's not a one hundred percent lie. I mean ... this is going to sound strange, but I hope you'll hear me out." Taking her hands, he gathered them into his. "The Russels ... we're not like any other family. First of all, we're, uh, wealthy. Very wealthy."

"Wealthy?" she echoed. "I mean, I kinda guessed that." He did have a nice place, and he could afford to fly his friends off to Vegas for the weekend on a private jet.

"Yeah, that's not all. In my pride, as with most lion prides, it's the women who have the power. They control the family assets and the business. The alpha—in this case, my sister—also gets to decide on alliances and has a big say on marriages."

"Wait a minute," she gasped. "Lions ... arrange marriages?"

"Er, kind of. It's not as bad as it sounds. No one gets married without either party's consent. But, couples are ... encouraged to get together. My father, for example, was from an Arizona pride a couple of hours away. His mother and my mother's mother got in touch when they were cubs and decided to introduce them. They spent summers together, and Dad was sent to the same university as Mom. Both of them knew the deal. It was how they were brought up. So, they let things just kind of develop from there.

"I swear, my father always told us he loved and adored my mother, and she loved him back. He was devoted and faithful to her up to the day they died. But they probably wouldn't have married if their parents hadn't approved the match in the first place."

"And you and Vicky?" she asked.

"I told you, our families were close. My sister's been our Alpha since I was a teenager, and so she was just ... following the way things have been done for generations. But I swear to you"—his hands tightened around her—"Vicky and I have never been engaged. Not before, and certainly not now."

"I know that," she said. "I couldn't believe all those lies she was spewing."

His face changed to that of relief. "You didn't?"

"Of course not," she said confidently. "Why should I believe the word of a mentally deranged heifer over the word of the man I love?" The words were out of her mouth so fast, she couldn't stop them. *Oh. Shit.*

Gabriel's eyes nearly popped out of their sockets. "W-what did you say?"

"*Eeep!*" Her hand slapped over her mouth. "I—" She spun around, trying to hide her flaming face from him. *OhGodohGodohGod.* "I didn't ..." It was too early to say that, wasn't it? "It just came out. I'm sor—"

"Don't you dare say you're sorry!" He spun her around so fast, she was dizzy. "Never ever say sorry, not about that. Look at me. Please, Temperance?"

Slowly, she lifted her head and looked into his eyes. They seemed even bluer now, shiny with what looked like tears.

"I love you, Temperance," he confessed. "My chest hurts so much from my heart wanting to burst out and say it to you. Scream it to the heavens so everyone can hear. You don't know how happy I am right now."

"Me too." She reached up and wrapped her arms around his neck, though he was already embracing her. His mouth found hers, their lips meeting in a soul-searing kiss. And that's what it felt like—a heat that surprisingly wasn't painful, unlike the fire that had scarred her. It was a strange sensation, slicing down her middle and pulling her apart before fusing her back together again. Whole, but not quite the same as she was moments before. When Gabriel pulled away, he looked at her, complete shock on his face.

"What's wrong?" she asked, reaching up to touch his cheek.

"I think ... I think that was the mating bond."

"Bond?" she exclaimed. "There's a mating bond?"

He nodded. "I didn't think ... I mean, I've heard about it but ..." Placing her hand on his chest, he covered it with his. "Feel my heartbeat, Temperance?" She did—strong and steady, following a steady rhythm. "This heart, it beats only for you. You're in here, with me. I can feel it. Can you?"

"I—" She felt dizzy again, and she had to lower her head for a moment and breathe deeply. Then she lifted her gaze to look at him—really look at him. The sun seemed to spark the highlights in his golden-blond hair, and his eyes were clearer than any winter morning sky she'd ever seen. It was like she had been smothered with a blanket her whole life, and now it was lifted off so she could see the world in a whole new way. Was this how he felt, too, when he looked at her? *Yes*, a new voice whispered inside her, banishing all the self-doubt from her mind and warming every dark and dreary part of her. "I can feel it."

The smile that spread on his face was more dazzling than any sunrise she'd seen. "Good. I love you, baby. Now, let's go home."

There was nothing she wanted more.

## Chapter 11

Gabriel watched Temperance in wonder as she slept in his arms. They were truly bonded and mated now, and he couldn't be more content. His lion roared with pride, too, then swished its tail back and forth smugly as if telling him, *I told you so.*

*You did, buddy,* he replied, happy for his animal to have this one. His arm tightened around her as he nuzzled her temple. She stirred, but didn't wake.

Yet despite it all, there was something bothering him, an inkling that things weren't as settled as they should be. Call it a gut instinct, but he had a feeling getting rid of Vicky had been almost too effortless. The lioness was never one to give up so easily, at least not without destroying as much as she could before she did eventually go down. The last apartment he rented had suffered so much damage, it had been cheaper to buy it from the landlord. He knew he would have to stay on his guard until he could find out if Vicky was going to retaliate so he could protect Temperance with everything he had.

Of course, it wasn't just Vicky he had to watch out for. There was the issue of his family, Gen in particular. It had been a relief that Temperance didn't believe in Vicky's lies, and that she didn't break up with him for keeping his family "tradition" a secret. He didn't mean to keep it from her, really, it was just he'd been too concentrated on winning her first. But the truth was, though Gen would find out one way or another, he couldn't dig up any fucks to give. Temperance was his mate, they were fully bonded, and no one could get in between them.

He caught a couple hours nap before it was time to get up again. After getting ready, he drove Temperance to the cafe and made plans to pick her up after five. He was unhappy about her car and house situation, but he knew she liked her independence and her job, too, so he wasn't going to push it. His lion, of course, was having none of that. It was urging him to move her into their den as soon as possible, but he wanted to let Temperance set the pace.

"Everything okay?" Damon asked when Gabriel walked into his office later that morning.

"Yeah. I just wanted you to be the first to know that Temperance and I bonded last night."

A rare smile spread across Damon's face. "Are you serious? Congratulations." He got up and rounded his desk to give Gabriel a quick hug and pat on the back. "Anna Victoria will be thrilled. Listen, I was thinking we should have dinner tonight. It'll give the girls a chance to get to know each other."

"Sounds great, but we can't stay out late," he said.

"I'll call Anna Victoria, and maybe we can meet on Main Street? How about Giorgio's at six thirty?"

"That should give me enough time to drive down and pick her up."

"Great. Anna Victoria's been dying to meet your Temperance."

*Your Temperance.* He had to admit, he liked the sound of

that. "Awesome, I gotta go start my patrol. See you later, man," he said, waving as he left the office.

Later, while on break, he called Temperance and managed to catch her on the phone to tell her about dinner.

"I don't know, Gabriel ..." she trailed off.

He didn't need to know why she was so apprehensive. "Damon's my best friend and Anna Victoria is his bonded mate. I really, really want them to meet you. But if you need some time, I understand. However, you should know that eventually, I'll have to introduce you to them."

"I ..." She paused. "All right. I'll meet you at the restaurant, is that okay? I wanna go home first and get dressed up."

"Whatever you need, baby," he said, feeling relieved. "See you there."

The rest of his shift was uneventful, and soon he was driving down to Main Street. Gabriel was the first one to arrive, but Anna Victoria and Damon were there, and to his surprise, J.D. was there too.

"We were doing wedding stuff," Anna Victoria said sheepishly. "I hope you don't mind that I invited J.D., too."

"I wanted to meet this genius who came up with that plan for Vegas," J.D. said with a chortle. "I can't believe you've been keeping her from us all this time."

"I wasn't," he said defensively. "But Temperance is shy and self-conscious." Actually, he was glad J.D. was here, too, at least he could explain everything to all of them in one go. So, he told them briefly about Temperance's scars without giving too much detail about her past. He'd just finished as Temperance walked through the door. "Here she is," he beamed as he strode to the door and put an arm around her. "Temperance, this is Damon and Anna Victoria. J.D. decided to join us as well."

"Hello," she said shyly, keeping the right side of her face

turned away from them. Though it hurt to see her have to hide, he knew he couldn't just push her to stop feeling self-conscious.

"It's nice to finally meet you," Damon said.

"Same here. And thank you," Anna Victoria added. "For thinking up that plan to have me come to the bachelor party."

J.D., in her usual brash manner, grabbed her left hand and tugged her away from Gabriel, and linked their arms together. "You're sitting next to me, Temperance. Gabriel's been hogging you for too long, and I haven't had any chance to tell you embarrassing stories about him."

"Hey!" Gabriel protested. "We're bonded, you can't scare her away anymore."

J.D. let out a laugh that sounded like a challenge. "Yeah, whatever. C'mon, I'm starving."

As dinner progressed, Temperance seemed to relax more which made Gabriel less tense. All of them accepted his mate, asking genuine questions about her and ensuring she was never left out when they told stories about the past or inside jokes.

"I'm glad to finally have someone else who's new to Blackstone," Anna Victoria said.

"Oh, did you just move here too?" Temperance asked as she took a sip of wine. "Why did you decide to move here?"

Anna Victoria went bright red. "Er, I didn't exactly decide," she said. "I just kind of ... arrived here."

"In a wedding dress," Gabriel added, unable to help himself. "After she jilted her previous groom."

"After *what?*" Temperance looked up at him for clarification.

"Don't make it sound so bad," Anna Victoria protested and then she told them the story of how she escaped her nasty fiancé from her arranged marriage, drove all the way to Blackstone, then walked into The Den in her wedding gown where she met Damon.

"Don't worry, buddy," Gabriel said. "I'll make sure she doesn't escape this Saturday."

"Yeah, you better, pretty boy," Damon warned jokingly.

"Speaking of which," Anna Victoria began. "Temperance, you'll come to our wedding this Saturday, right? I mean, Gabriel's asked you to be his date?"

"Er ..." She looked up at him, her light hazel eyes going wide.

"I haven't, actually," he said. "And that's my mistake. Will you be my date, Temperance?"

"I don't know," she whispered.

"But you have to come, Temperance," J.D. whined.

"I don't have anything to wear," she said.

"It's not a formal dress type of affair," Anna Victoria said. "After the church, we're having a barbecue at the Blackstone Castle grounds. I didn't want anything fussy or fancy."

"I'll lend you something to wear," J.D. offered. "No wait, scratch that. I only own one dress, and I'll be wearing it as maid of honor. But I'll go shopping with you."

"Me too," Anna Victoria said.

"It'll be great, Temperance," he assured her. "And I'd really like it if you were there." He could already picture it in his mind. Sitting next to her at the ceremony. Holding her hand while they walked into reception. Dancing with her under the stars. "Please?"

Four pairs of eyes looked at her hopefully. "I ..." She nodded. "All right."

"Yes!" J.D. exclaimed and grabbed her phone from her pocket. "Give me your number, and we'll go shopping this week."

"Wow, you should be honored. J.D. hates shopping for clothes," Damon joked.

"Only when I'm shopping for myself," she shot back.

"Thank you," Gabriel whispered into her ear. "I promise, if you don't feel comfortable at all, we can leave anytime."

"It's fine," she said, looking up at him with a smile on her face. "And you can't leave, you're the best man."

"And you're my mate." He kissed her on the tip of her nose. "You're always going to be my priority."

A pretty blush spread over her face. "Thank you."

———

Most of the week was uneventful, and soon, Saturday rolled around. They had the ceremony at St. John's Chapel in Blackstone. Damon was not very fond of crowds, so only his parents and a select few people were at the church, including Gabriel and Temperance.

"I'm glad the ceremony went well," Temperance said as they stood with the guests outside the church, waiting for the bride and groom to exit. "Was there any problem? Why were Anna Victoria and J.D. late?"

The ceremony had started thirty minutes later because the bridal car didn't arrive on time. "According to J.D., there was some drama about the dress," Gabriel said. "But I guess they fixed it; they just needed some extra time."

The doors of the church flew open, and as Damon and Anna Victoria stepped out, they were greeted with a shower of rice and rose petals. The groom looked handsome in his tux, while Anna Victoria was radiant in her blush peach gown.

"Well, she—they look perfect," she said as they watched the bride and groom get into the Mercedes waiting at the end of the driveway, a "Just Married" sign hanging from the back.

"You're perfect," he said, pulling her into his arms and growling against her lips. "In case I forgot to tell you."

Her cheeks went pink. "You have Anna Victoria and J.D. to

thank for the outfit and my makeup and hair."

"You do look beautiful, but it's not just that. *You* are perfect." She was wearing a simple yellow dress with sleeves made of a delicate translucent fabric that covered her arms, but looked comfortable and elegant at the same time, while her hair was styled so that a few tendrils of hair covered her cheek, but not fully. He reminded himself to thank Anna Victoria and J.D. for whatever they did to help Temperance feel less insecure about her scars.

"We should go to the reception," she said. "J.D. said she needs some help setting out the party favors."

They made their way to Blackstone Castle in his Jeep, and soon, he was pulling up to the massive driveway in front.

"Wow, it really is a castle," Temperance exclaimed. "Have you been inside?"

"Yeah," he said. "I've been a couple times. Damon and I were the same year as Jason and Matthew Lennox, so we were invited to their birthday parties and other events." Not to mention, his mother had sat on the board of the Lennox Foundation, and liked rubbing elbows with the Blackstone dragons. When he was a teenager, Geraldine Russel had hinted that he should ask Sybil Lennox to the prom, which he promptly ignored. The youngest and only female Lennox was not even in high school then, plus, he did not want to face the wrath of three—which included their adoptive brother, Luke Lennox—protective older brothers, two of whom could breathe fire. "I'm sure we can poke around later. Maybe I can show you that closet where we used to play seven minutes in heaven," he said, waggling his eyebrows at her.

"It's Damon and Anna Victoria's wedding," she reminded him with a chuckle.

"So? What do you think they'll be doing tonight?"

She slapped him playfully on the chest. "C'mon, J.D. said to meet her by the refreshment table."

Special rope fences and markers had been set up to lead guests around the castle to the massive grounds in the back. There was a huge stone and marble patio where tables and chairs and the dance floor were set up, while three industrial-sized barbecue pits were placed on the lawn just below the patio, along with several tables laden with sides and desserts. The snow-capped Blackstone Mountains made for a spectacular backdrop for the whole affair, and Gabriel couldn't help but think what a fitting place this was for his best friend to celebrate his wedding.

The bride and groom arrived shortly after them, and soon the guests were coming in. As Anna Victoria requested, she did not want any pomp or fuss around the reception, so she and Damon mingled amongst their guests as they pleased, then opened the dance floor when the sun was beginning to set and everyone had their fill of food, cake, and wine.

Gabriel danced with Temperance three times before he relented and released her to Damon. J.D. took the opportunity to partner with him.

"C'mon," she said, tugging at his hand. "Before Anders finds me again and starts ragging on me about this dress."

"Well, I wouldn't blame him," he said, glancing down at her outfit. J.D. looked ... well, different. Okay, she was beautiful, but he only thought that because he'd never seen her in anything other than T-shirts, jeans, and overalls, and now she wore a green and blue strapless dress that showed off her curves. Her blonde hair was tamed into waves that hung loosely down her shoulders, and she was actually wearing makeup. "Weren't you two good buddies in Vegas?"

"Ha! I only hung out with him because I wanted to keep Damon from killing him *and* so he would spend more money on the strippers," she said. "I hope those girls bought themselves something nice with all the money he spent. And—" She frowned and her back stiffened.

"What's wrong?"

She twisted him around so he faced outwards, away from the castle. "Your two o'clock. There's someone in the shadows."

Swinging his head around, he used his shifter vision to focus in the line of trees at the edge of the lawn. A large silhouette stood still between the shrubs, unmoving. His lion, however, was not alarmed. "Don't worry," he assured her. "I think I know who that is."

"Who?" J.D. asked.

"Krieger," he said.

Her nose wrinkled. "Who's that?"

"An old friend of Damon's."

"Huh." Spinning their positions around, she glanced behind him toward where Krieger was. "Then why is he hiding out there?"

He thought back to when he first saw the bear shifter. "Oh, that's right, you never met him. He's an old army buddy of Damon's, and we all went through training together. He's a good guy, he just doesn't like being around people." Gabriel guessed that the former master sergeant probably wanted to be here, but couldn't bring himself to come forward. He couldn't blame the guy. Though he didn't know the entire story, apparently, he'd gone through an even rougher time than Damon.

"Maybe we should ask him to come out? We have lots of food."

"Nah, we'll just scare him off." His brows furrowed. "It's weird though, he never ventures farther than his patrol area, and that's all the way up in Contessa Peak. I wonder—"

"Gabriel! Why the hell haven't you been answering your phone?"

He abruptly stopped dancing as he felt a punch on his

shoulder. Releasing J.D., he turned to see Ginny standing behind him, hands on her hips, cheeks puffing from exertion. "Gin? What are you doing here?"

"I've been trying to call you for hours. Why haven't you been picking up?" his sister cried.

"I turned it off for the ceremony and forgot to turn it back on. What's wrong?"

"What's wrong? I—shit! I'm too late!" She pointed her chin back at the castle. "They're here."

"Who?" He followed Ginny's gaze. "Oh, *fuck*."

"What the hell is going on, Russel?" J.D. asked, hands splayed on her hips.

"Vicky's here," he groaned. "And she's not alone." No, she definitely was not. Gen and his other sister Gemma were with her, as well as William Woolworth, Vicky's dad.

"That crazy harpy is here?" J.D.'s eyes glowed. The only person who hated Vicky more than Ginny was J.D., because the lioness always thought the mechanic had designs on Gabriel herself. Pushing her non-existent sleeves up, she gritted her teeth. "I'm going to knock her—"

"No, J.D.," he sighed. "This is a family matter." Now it was anyway, because Vicky had brought his two oldest sisters into the picture. "Please, can you just make sure nothing happens out here? I don't want them to ruin Damon and Anna Victoria's wedding." That thought enraged him more than Vicky tattling on him to Gen, which he assumed was the reason they were all here crashing the reception. "I'll get rid of them right away."

"I—Fine," J.D.'s eyes returned to normal. "But if she gets near me, Anna Victoria, or Damon, I'm going to claw her eyes out." Pivoting on her heel, she marched toward the bar.

He stalked toward the doorway that led into the castle, Ginny hot on his heels. Vicky and her father were standing there, as well as his sisters, *and* Matthew Lennox who was looking cool and collected, though his body language was protective as he moved between them and the reception area.

"... can I offer you some wine? Or anything else?" Matthew said diplomatically.

"That's not necessary, and I do apologize for intruding, Matthew," Gen began, her blonde brows drawn into a frown. "I didn't—"

"What are you doing here?" Gabriel groused. His lion, too, was not happy as it chuffed and flicked its ears. "Matthew, I'm so sorry. They"—he flashed Vicky a venomous look—"were definitely not invited."

"We just needed to talk to Gabriel about an important family matter," Vicky said.

Matthew gestured behind them. "If you need some privacy, please feel free to use the inner patio," he said. Though it sounded like a suggestion, coming from the Blackstone Dragon, it was really more like a directive. Even Gabriel's lion understood and backed off.

"Of course, thank you again, Matthew," Gen said with a deferent nod.

They all marched into the inner patio, and as soon as Matthew closed the door behind him, Gabriel exploded. "Are you fucking serious?" he shouted at Vicky. "Are you trying to ruin Damon's wedding?"

"You left me no choice," she said. "I couldn't believe you would dare choose her over me."

"I would choose her—or anyone else—a thousand times over you, you thoughtless witch!"

"Can someone please explain what's going on?" Gen said calmly. "I do *not* like having my time wasted."

Gabriel whirled to face her. "You don't know why you're here?"

Gemma answered. "We were supposed to have a business

dinner with William." She nodded at the older balding man next to Vicky. "He was insistent on tonight, and then he led us here. I thought maybe he had something up his sleeve with Lennox."

"I'm sorry to, uh, lure you here under less than honest circumstances," William began. "But perhaps it was better you see it for yourselves."

"See what?" Gen asked, annoyed.

"That your brother has been screwing around with a *human*," Vicky exclaimed.

"Is this true, Gabriel?" Gen's gaze narrowed at him. "Is this why you've been avoiding my calls?"

"I—" He blew out a breath. "It's not what you think."

"I've never meddled in your little flings," Gen began. "But you know you have a duty to your family. You're a Russel, Gabriel, and that means responsibilities."

"Responsibility has never been his strong suit," Gemma said with a roll of her eyes. He and his second-oldest sister had an even more contentious relationship than his one with Gen. "That's going to change soon." She glanced at William and Vicky.

"You don't understand," Gabriel began. "She—"

"Son, you know how this goes," William said gently. "Your father, God rest his soul, understood our ways."

Vicky's smile turned sickly sweet. "And you know what that means."

"I'm never going to marry you, Vicky," he spat. "And you can't keep me away from Temperance."

Gen harrumphed. "Gabriel, you must break things with her now. William and I want to begin negotiations about a possibly buyout of his company, and we both agreed"—she nodded at the older man, who returned the gesture—"things would be smoother if we had other ... alliances in order first."

Ginny snorted. "Good luck with that. Woolworth Inc.'s losing money faster than Ol' William here is losing his hair."

"What do you mean?" Gemma asked.

"Oh, I exist now, huh?" Ginny shot back. She had an even more volatile relationship with Gemma than he did. "Let's see ... when I heard that Vicky here has been trying to speed up her walk down the aisle, I did a little digging and found Woolworth's financial statements—the real ones he didn't want to show you. And things aren't looking as rosy as they seem, are they?" she said to William, who instantly turned bright red. "I think that last expansion did you in. Couldn't keep up with your creditors."

Gemma's eyes turned into razor-thin slits. "I think we may have to go back to the negotiating table."

"We'll settle this later, William," Gen said to the older Woolworth as she shot him with a freezing glare. "In any case, Gabriel," she began, turning back to him. "You know you can't keep this relationship with this ... human." Her lips twisted distastefully.

"I will not break up with Temperance," he said.

"I'm sure we can work this out, Gen," Vicky pleaded. "You have to make him listen to you—"

"Shut the hell up, Vicky." Gabriel faced his sisters, hands curling into fists. "Because I won't give up Temperance. She's my mate, and we've already bonded."

The complete silence that followed his statement was deafening, broken only by a shriek.

"*Mate?*" Vicky cried. "No! That's not true. There's no such thing."

"She's your mate?" Gemma said. "A human?"

"You know it's not farfetched. Matthew and Jason Lennox's mates are human," he said to Gen. "I swear to you, it's true,

Gen. She and I are bonded now, and if you try to split us up, I swear to God—"

"Stop!" She held a hand up, her lips thinning as she pulled them back in with a grimace. With a sigh, she massaged the bridge of her nose. "If this is true, then ... then we must respect the mate bond."

William turned even redder. "You can't believe this nonsense," he sputtered.

"My brother may be many things, William, but he's not a liar." William opened his mouth but clamped it shut when the Alpha lioness narrowed her razor-sharp gaze at him. "We should head back home. We've caused enough of a disturbance."

"I'll have our lawyers call yours," Gemma added.

"You bastard!" Vicky railed at Gabriel. "How dare you!"

"Excuse me?" he said.

"I should have gotten rid of her myself." Vicky's face twisted into an expression of hate. "Instead of leaving it to incompetent *males!*"

"Vicky, pumpkin," William said nervously, placing a hand on her shoulder. "Let's—"

"No!" She whirled around. "You said you'd take care of her! That that ex-boyfriend of hers would drag her back to whatever hellhole—"

"What?" White-hot rage coursed through Gabriel as he focused his gaze on father and daughter. "What the hell is she saying?" His tone was dead serious.

"Nothing," William gulped.

Gabriel lunged forward, grabbing the old man by his collar. "You have two seconds to tell me the truth, old man."

"Gabriel!"

He ignored Gen's warning shout. "Tell me!"

William turned pale. "V-Vicky told me about your-your

human, and so I had her followed and investigated. My PI found Mr. Morello and ... persuaded him to come here so he could convince Miss Pettigrew to leave Blackstone."

Gabriel could guess how Tony was 'persuaded.' "You motherfucker. He could have hurt her!"

"He was an idiot druggie who only wanted money," Vicky spat. "When he failed the first time, he kept coming back around, promising he'd take care of her, one way or another. He hasn't stopped harassing me, and he's been blowing up my father's phone all day, messaging him that 'today was the day,' and we better have his cash ready."

Vicky's words suddenly made the blood freeze in Gabriel's brain and his lion's hackles rose. He suddenly remembered his encounter with Temperance's ex last week and the desperation in the other man's eyes. "Fuck!"

"What's wrong?" Ginny asked. "Hey! Where are you—"

Gabriel rushed back out to the patio, his eyes scanning the guests.

He didn't know why, but he felt ... something was wrong. Like he could feel fear and anxiety coming from somewhere, but he couldn't say where.

*Please, oh please, oh please let that feeling be wrong.*

His stomach turned to lead as he realized that Temperance was nowhere in sight. The last time he saw her was when she danced with Damon, but he saw his friend was now sitting at the sweethearts' table with his new wife. "Damn it!"

Panic and terror tore through him. He knew, he just knew she was in trouble. Like he was feeling what she was feeling.

He rounded the castle, heading out to the front. Cars lined the driveway, but there was no one else there. *Where could he have taken her?*

When the smell of gasoline hit his nose, he let out an enraged roar.

## Chapter 12

Temperance had been enjoying herself at the reception immensely, much more than she thought she would. While she had been nervous all week about attending the wedding, J.D. and Anna Victoria had helped make her feel welcome into their little group. Of course, spending time with Gabriel and having him assure her of his love and support the whole time had also boosted her confidence. She wanted for him to be proud of her, and also, she thought maybe it was time to stop hiding herself—and her scars. A few people had stared at her cheek and hands, and though it still bothered her, she didn't feel as self-conscious as before.

And now here she was, dancing with the groom in front of everyone. But she was eager to go back to her mate. As soon as the song ended, Temperance glanced around. "Huh, I don't see Gabriel."

"I'm sure he's around somewhere," Damon said as he released her hand. "Why don't I keep you company while you wait for him to come back?"

"Don't be silly, Damon." She pointed her chin toward the sweethearts' table where Anna Victoria was sitting by herself.

"Your bride needs you. Now, scoot," she gave him a gentle push, though he didn't need any more encouragement to join his mate.

Glancing around her and seeing that Gabriel was still nowhere in sight, she decided to head to the ladies' room to freshen up. Signs and solar-powered torches had been put up that led to the pool area off to the side of the great lawn, which had been set up to accommodate guests. As she walked the makeshift path, a stiff breeze made her shiver. Rubbing her hands on her arms, she felt something else, and it wasn't just the crisp spring air.

"Tempe."

Gooseflesh rose on her skin. "What—*mmmph!*"

A hand clamped over her mouth as she felt herself hauled against a hard, male chest. "Don't scream, Tempe." Tony's sour breath made her want to gag and she tried to wiggle out of his arms. "Don't make me use this."

Something sharp poked at her side. *A knife.* She immediately stopped struggling.

"That's it, good girl."

A muffled whimper tried to escape her mouth, but his grip tightened. "C'mon, Tempe baby. Just relax." He pushed her through the line of trees at the edge of the lawn, away from sight. When she attempted to drag her feet, he only pressed the knife deeper into her rib, slicing through the delicate fabric of the dress. She winced as she felt the sharp tip draw blood.

Helpless, she allowed him to lead her along the length of the reception area, her heart plummeting with each step as she watched the revelry of the wedding going on, no one the wiser as to what was happening in the shadows. She thought she heard the snap of a twig, but it must have been a small animal.

Finally, they slipped to the side of the castle and to the driveway where all the cars were parked. Tony dragged her along the gravel path to the bottom of the hill where his rusted-out sedan was parked in the middle of the driveway. He pushed her inside the passenger side and slammed the door shut.

Immediately, she went for the handle, but realized it had been sawed off. Frantically, she searched the other doors, hopping over to the back seat, but they too had their handles removed, as well as the locking mechanisms. "Let me out!" she screamed, slamming her palms on the glass.

"You should have just gone with me, Tempe," Tony said, his voice sounding hollow. "I told you I'd find a way."

What was he saying? "You can't kidnap me!" she cried. "Do you think this is going to make me take you back? Make me love you?"

"Hah!" he sneered. "You think I want you back after you fucked that animal? No way. I might get some disease from you."

"Then what do you want?" she asked. "I don't have any money." And there was no way she was going to let him extort money from Gabriel.

"I know that," he said. "But someone else promised me big bucks to get rid of you." He scratched at his arms with his dirty fingers. When her gaze lowered, he immediately dropped his hands.

*Oh, how did I miss that?* The track marks. The twenty pounds he seemed to have dropped. The general unkemptness and lack of hygiene. Her mother and stepfather had been the same. And since she'd stopped being intimate with Tony months before they broke up, she hadn't seen his naked arms in a while. "Tony, please," she said. "Let me go, and we can get some help."

"I don't need help," he hissed. "Not after tonight." Stalking over to the trunk, he opened it and hauled something large out.

"To—" *No.*

He lifted a gasoline can over his head. "I told that bitch and her father, today was the day I was going to get rid of you."

"Tony, please!" She rapped her fists at the windows. "No!"

But it was no use. Tony uncapped the can and began sloshing the liquid out onto the car. The pungent smell of petroleum and ether hit her nose, making her gag. When she saw the lighter in his hand, she pressed her body as far away from his as possible. It was the last thing she saw before she was blinded by the blaze that lit up in front of her eyes.

In a split second she felt a myriad of emotions. Fear yes, as the memories came back. But also a desperation and anxiety surging inside her, coming from somewhere else.

The atmosphere grew around her, and she raised her arms to cover her face. Smoke was now starting to fill the inside of the car, and she closed her eyes to stop them from tearing up.

*Oh God, this was it.* She was going to die in this blaze, and her first thought was of Gabriel. She would never see his handsome face or—

The car shook violently, knocking her around on the back seat. Gripping the headrest, she hung on as the ear-splitting sound of metal being ripped apart nearly tore her eardrums. When it stopped, she opened one eye and gasped as she realized the entire roof had been shredded. Something large loomed overhead, then a massive animal's head lowered.

Fear, hope, and relief surged through her, all at the same time.

She should have been scared by the sight of the lion above her, its giant maw gaping and teeth bared, but she knew who it was. Something stirred in her soul that whispered, *Gabriel.* Immediately, she sprang up and grabbed onto the lion's neck. Her feet lifted off the back seat, and it was like she was flying, albeit for only a few seconds.

"Oomph!" Air rushed out of her lungs as she landed on

something firm, but it wasn't the ground as she felt fur under her. The lion had twisted them around so it hit the gravel instead of her. "Oh, Gabriel!" She scrambled to her feet and brushed her hair out of her face.

The lion rolled around and got up on all four paws, shaking its mighty mane and letting out an annoyed roar as it accidentally snorted a piece of ash into its nostrils. She couldn't help the giggle as the animal looked adorable, and she reached out to pat away some singeing on the tips of its mane. "There now," she said as it licked her fingers gratefully with its rough tongue. "Hey now! Stop, that tickles."

Stepping backwards, the lion kept its glowing gaze on her as its muscles began to shift under its furry skin. Its limbs began to shorten, and its mane receded back, as did its mighty snout. As the lion shifted back into its human form, she never broke its gaze, staring deep into its sky-blue eyes until Gabriel stood before her.

"Temperance," he breathed, his voice breaking as the glow dissipated from his eyes. "I—"

She launched herself at him. "Gabriel ... oh, Gabriel."

He lifted her up into his arms in a crushing embrace. "I thought I'd lost you. It was like, I could feel you were scared and then I couldn't find you."

"Me too," she said. "I mean, it's strange. Like I knew you were worried for me." Could it be that bond they shared? "I didn't think I'd see you again. That I was going to—"

"Shhh." He stopped her with his lips. "You're fine now. Everything's fine."

"I was going to the bathroom and Tony—" She inhaled a sharp breath. "Tony! He tried to kill me and—" She glanced around. "Did he get away?"

Gabriel's face broke into an angry scowl. "I saw him run." He set her down and dashed toward the trees.

She followed him, despite not knowing where to go. "Gabriel!" she called, scrambling in the darkness.

A loud growl echoed through the forest, and a bone-chilling scream followed. The ground seemed to vibrate, and she immediately stopped, her heart banging against her chest like a sledgehammer. "Gab—"

"I'm here, baby!" Strong arms wrapped around her as Gabriel's familiar scent tickled her nose. "I'm here, we're safe. You're safe."

She pushed her face into his chest. "Oh my God, I thought you ... and he ...'"

"It wasn't me," he said. "Tony ... ran into someone else."

"Who?"

"An old friend." He kissed the top of her head. "Anyway, it doesn't matter. Tony won't be bothering us anymore."

Her arms tightened around him. "Gabriel ..."

"I thought I was going to lose you," he murmured against her hair. "I'm sorry I wasn't there to protect you."

"But you saved me," she said. "And everything's going to be all right."

"Yes, baby," he promised. "From now on, everything will be all right."

And she believed him.

## Epilogue
### THREE MONTHS LATER ...

Gabriel let out a satisfied breath as he punched his time card to end his shift for the very last time. "And it's official," he said to no one in particular. Today was his final day with the Blackstone Rangers.

Sentiment ran through him, and some sadness, too. This place had been his second home, after all, and in some ways, what had started him on this path that led to his fate. The Blackstone Rangers would always have a special place in his heart, but now that particular organ—and his soul—belonged to his mate.

Damon had been disappointed when he gave his notice a few weeks ago. "I'll miss seeing you around every day, man," he had said. "But I understand."

The schedule had been taking its toll on him, even though he moved Temperance in with him two weeks after Damon and Anna Victoria's wedding. She had protested at first, but it was driving him crazy knowing she almost died that night. Of course, he didn't have to worry about that bastard seeing as Krieger had taken care of him—something he still hadn't thanked the bear shifter for.

Vicky and William were still in the picture, though he had filed restraining orders against father and daughter. They were also facing charges for solicitation to commit kidnapping, but it still didn't settle him and his lion. They had a big row over it, but after they sat down and talked, Temperance relented. They packed up her trailer, and she—and Fred, of course—moved into his loft.

Still, their shifts didn't jive. When he would come home after his usual day shift at ten at night, she could barely stay awake. He'd wake up early to bring her to work and stay with her until it was time for his shift, but she was so absorbed while she worked, they didn't really spend much time together. So, he knew something had to change and since Temperance loved her job, he decided to quit. However, not wanting to leave Damon in a lurch, he agreed to stay on part-time for a couple of weeks, with the understanding that he could clock out as early as he wanted.

"Yo, Russel!" Anders came up to him and slapped him on the shoulder. "So that's it huh? You're leaving us?" He flashed him a mock hurt expression. "I guess someone has to count the gold coins in your vault, huh?"

"Yeah, whatever, Stevens." Despite being an asshole, Gabriel would always be grateful to Anders for letting him swap shifts so he could spend more time with Temperance.

"Seriously though, what are you gonna do now? Go into the family business?"

He would rather have his balls strung up, which frankly wasn't far off from what would happen if he did take a job at Lyon Industries. "I'll get by," he said. Actually, he already had a plan, but he would need to discuss it with Temperance first. "Say, what are you doing here anyway? Your shift doesn't start until later."

"I haven't left, man. Not since I came in last night." He

nodded at the crowd of people waiting outside the HQ doors. "Not with all the added visitors we've been getting. Told the chief I needed a couple of hours to get away from this craziness."

*Right.* "Damon's about ready to have an aneurysm, but it's good publicity. If you need a break, come down to Rosie's with me. I'll get you dinner."

The tiger shifter's face brightened. "Really? You never bought me dinner before. All right, you don't have to ask me twice."

They drove down to Main Street separately and were soon walking into the front door of Rosie's. The place was packed, but it was summer and high tourist season, not to mention, the exciting events of two weeks ago had put Blackstone on the map, so the town was seeing double the usual amount of visitors. When Rosie saw them, however, she immediately waved at them and ushered them into an empty booth.

"I'll let Temperance know you're here," she said as she filled their mugs with coffee. "So, I'll get you a slice each of our specials? We have cherry lemon, dragonfruit, and something Temperance calls Bear-y Hero pie, which is basically blueberry, strawberries, and boysenberries."

Anders groaned. "I thought I could get away from that hero shit—er, stuff," he corrected himself when Rosie sent him a warning lift of her brow.

Gabriel laughed. "I'll have one of each, but Anders will have the first two."

"Coming right up," Rosie said as she pivoted on her heel and walked away.

"So," Anders began. "How are—"

"Excuse me," the woman in the next booth turned her head to face them, "but are you guys rangers?" Her gaze dropped down to their khaki uniforms.

Anders's face immediately perked up at the female attention. "This guy"—he jerked his thumb at Gabriel—"isn't anymore, but I am." He wiggled a brow at her. "What can I do for you, sweetheart?"

The woman slid out from the booth and pivoted toward them. Her long, caramel hair was pulled back into a ponytail, and she wore high heels, tight ripped jeans, and a lacy sleeveless top that showed off the tattoos on her arm. "I was wondering, do you guys know where I can find Daniel Rogers?"

Anders groaned and slunk lower in the booth. "I'm so *fucking* tired of hearing that name."

Gabriel rolled his eyes. "Sorry about my friend, he's a drama king. Can I ask why you need to know where he is?"

She folded her arms over her chest as her razor-sharp gaze cut into him. "You could."

Seconds ticked by, and Gabriel, feeling impatient, shrugged. "He should be at HQ—that's the Blackstone Rangers Headquarters. It's on the road that leads up to the mountains, you can't miss it."

"Thank you."

She dropped some bills on her table, and as she turned to walk away, Anders called after her. "Hey, baby, what do you need him for when I'm here? Those tats are a piece of art, you know." He nodded at her arm. "And so are you. Maybe I can—"

"Nail me to the wall?" she scoffed. "Please. Like I haven't heard that one before." Pivoting on her heel, she sauntered off, hips swinging as she walked away from them.

"What do you think she wants with Rogers?" Gabriel asked.

"What else? Everyone wants a piece of Blackstone's newest celebrity," Anders groused. "She doesn't look like a reporter, so maybe a groupie? Fuck me, if I had known saving the vice president's life would have chicks crawling over each other to get to me, I'd have jumped on that stage myself."

A few days ago, the vice president had come for an official visit to Blackstone, a first for the shifter town. Gabriel didn't know the politics of the visit, but everyone had come out to welcome Vice President Scott Baker with a parade and then a speech at Lennox Park. For obvious reasons, security was ramped up, and the PD had asked the rangers to come for backup and help with crowd control.

During the speech, a man had somehow broken through the barriers and attempted to shoot the VP. Rogers had been in the right place at the right time and took the would-be assassin down before he could kill Baker. Needless to say, his heroic act had garnered national attention, and footage of him tackling the gunman to the ground played on every single news station in the country, sending Rogers to new heights of fame as his picture was splashed on every newspaper, magazine, and social media sites. Reporters flooded the town, not to mention enthusiastic fans of the newly-crowned hero, which was the reason why the mountains in particular had been teeming with visitors as they hoped to catch a glimpse of the normally camera-shy Rogers.

"Jesus." Anders' eyes grew wide, his mouth dropping open.

"What?" he asked.

"I just remembered why I thought she looked familiar."

"She?"

"That broad looking for Rogers." He snapped his fingers. "She was *there*. At the strip club in Vegas. I'm sure of it."

"Strip club? She's a stripper?" Gabriel wouldn't have recognized her as he had done his best not to look at the women than night.

Anders guffawed. "Nah. One of the girls at the bachelorette party next to us," he said. "I can't forget those tats. And ... I may have given her the same pickup line," he added sheepishly.

"You never were original," Gabriel drolled.

A line furrowed between Anders's brows. "Hmmm. I never

did tell you, did I? Rogers disappeared on us that night, and we didn't see him again until it was time to leave the next day. Nearly missed the plane ride home."

"He did? Where did he go?"

"Said he couldn't recall what happened. Just woke up in some motel room on the Strip. Shit, I didn't think he had that much to drink." Shifters could get drunk, but it took a lot of alcohol. "Anyway, what do you think she—oh, fuck me!" The tiger shifter barked out a laugh and slapped his palm on the table, making several of the other diners send them dirty looks.

"What's the matter with you?" Gabriel asked.

"Holy mother of—" Anders's face spread into a grin. "Do you think she's ..."

"She's what?"

"You *know*." He made a rounding gesture with his hand over his stomach. "Knocked up?"

"What?" Daniel getting a random one-night stand pregnant? "No way." He couldn't believe it. But then again, if he had been so drunk he couldn't remember it ...

"Here are your pies, gentlemen."

The sound of the familiar voice made him and his lion perk up. Temperance stood next to the booth, tray in hand. "You're a sight for sore eyes," he said, his eyes roaming over her gorgeous form.

The smile that spread across her face lit up the room. "Rosie told me you'd arrived. And I thought I'd come over and bring these to you myself. Hey, Anders," she greeted. "Wait, where are you going?" she asked when the tiger shifter got to his feet.

"No offense, Temperance, I love your baking. But I'm not gonna stay here while you two make goo-goo eyes at each other." He looked at Gabriel knowingly. "Besides, you know I wanna be there and see Roger's stupid fucking face when she walks into that door. See ya guys later."

"What is he talking about?" Temperance asked as she watched Anders dash out of the cafe.

Gabriel sighed. "I'll tell you later. For now ..." He grabbed the tray from her and placed it on the table, then took her hand and planted her on his lap. "I missed you," he said, nuzzling at her neck.

She sighed. "There are people here. They're staring at us."

"So?" He kissed her square on the mouth. "Let them stare."

"Gabriel ..." she warned, but kissed him back, then scrambled off his lap. He scooted over so she could sit next to him. "So, it's done?" she said. "No more shifts?"

"Yeah," he said. "I told Damon I'd be happy to help if they're shorthanded, but he says he'll manage. Said he's thinking of hiring help from the outside since the new batch of trainees aren't done yet."

"Are you sure this is what you want?" she asked in a quiet voice. "I'd hate to think you quit because of me."

"Oh, baby." He took her hand and brushed his lips against her knuckles. "I told you, I wasn't cut out for that job anyway." In truth, he'd been thinking about leaving as soon as Damon started to settle with Anna Victoria. He had originally joined to support his friend, but now he was doing fine on his own with the help of his mate.

"What are you going to do now?" she asked. "Are you going to work for your sisters?"

He didn't need to work at all, but he wasn't the type to lay about and do nothing. "Actually, I wanted to talk to you about that." From across the room, he caught Rosie's eye. The fox shifter smiled at him and gave him a nod. "I've been talking to Rosie, actually."

"You have?"

"Yeah. See, she's been thinking of taking it easy. Stepping back a bit."

"Huh. She did mention that she needed a vacation."

"Yeah, so ..." He took a deep breath. "I offered to buy her out."

"What?" she asked incredulously. "You're going to buy Rosie's?"

He nodded. "Yeah. She's been wanting to retire for a while now, but she didn't want to just hand over the business to anyone," he said. "She wants someone she can trust, who'll take care of this place and love it as much as she does, but also bring new life into it. Baby, she wants *you*."

"I ..." Her breath caught in her throat as her head swung around to meet Rosie's gaze. The older woman looked at them warmly, affection evident in her eyes. "I don't know ..."

"It's not gonna happen right now, maybe not soon," he said. "But, how about it? We can be partners."

"Partners?"

He nodded. "You and me. What do you say?"

She looked deep in thought for a moment, then said, "Of course, I mean, yes. Thank you." She reached out to wrap her arms around him, embracing him tightly.

"Thank God," he said. "That means I don't have to go back to the rangers and pretend I'm not dying inside when I see toads and frogs." He gave an exaggerated shiver.

She chuckled. "You know I'll protect you from those evil slimy adorable monsters," she said. "It's my job as your mate, you know?"

Warmth filled him he looked at her beautiful face, feeling the bond between them that had been growing stronger each day. He pushed a lock of hair that had fallen into her eyes, his fingertips brushing the marred skin of her cheek. She didn't blink, flinch, or even turn away. In fact, in the last few months, the scars didn't seem to bother her as much. Today, she wasn't even self-conscious about going out into the dining room full of people wearing a shirt that left her arms bare and her hair tied back into a ponytail away from her pretty face.

He licked off a spot of flour from her nose. "You know, I'm really glad you, J.D., and Anna Victoria have become good friends," he began. The two other women had fully embraced his mate, and they hung out and went shopping all the time. "I still haven't thanked them for whatever it is they're doing to make you feel more comfortable about yourself."

Her head cocked to the side. "Anna Victoria and J.D.? Oh, Gabriel." She reached up and cupped the side of his face. "It wasn't that," she said. "I mean, yeah, I do feel comfortable around them, and they've been great friends. But the reason I've been feeling less self-conscious is ..." She took a deep breath. "It's you, Gabriel. When I look at your face, into your eyes, I see the way you see me. Like there's nothing wrong with me."

"There's not," he said flatly. "It's the way I've always seen you."

Her eyes misted. "I know," she said, her voice choking. "Now I know."

The bond hummed between them again, and he couldn't help himself as he reached for her and pressed his mouth to hers. Later tonight, when they were alone in bed after they made love, he would tell her, too. Tell her that when he looked into her eyes, he saw the love reflected there that made him feel like he was more than just a shallow charmer, a rich pretty boy that was suitable only for one purpose. In her eyes, he was a man worthy of her love. He would ask her, too, to be his forever, not just in the eyes of their kind, but in the eyes of everyone so there would be no doubt in anyone's mind they belonged together. *I'm going to marry you so hard, Temperance Pettigrew, just you wait and see.* But for now ...

"I'm starving," he said, pulling away. "Let's eat."

———

Dear Reader,

Thank you so much for reading Temperance and Gabriel's journey.

Want to read a sexy bonus scene TOO HOT to publish? Subscribe to my newsletter now and get access.

Now, what exactly happened during the bachelor party in Vegas?

And who is this mystery lady looking for Daniel?

(More important—why does she need to talk to him?)

Find out when Blackstone Ranger Hero comes out in early September.

Pre-order it now, while it's only $2.99 (goes up to 3.99 on release day)

All my love,

Alicia

P.S. If you don't want to sign up for my newsletter, just join my Facebook group!

"C'mon Rogers, don't be such a pussy!"

Daniel Rogers breathed a sigh and took a sip of his beer. "I think you guys are doing just fine without me," he shouted over the loud din of the music pumping through the speakers.

Anders Stevens rolled his eyes. "Seriously? You're not going to play? Not even one lousy dollar for those hardworking girls up there?"

He lifted his head an inch, forcing himself to look at the three scantily-clad women on stage. One of them, wearing only sparkly nipple covers and a G-string hung upside down from a pole. "They certainly are ... talented."

"Yeah, very *big* talents," Anders added with a waggle of his eyebrow. "Look, the groom-to-be and Russel,"—he jerked a thumb at the back of the room to where their two other companions, Damon Cooper and Gabriel Russel, were huddled by the buffet table—"aren't going to be participating in the festivities anytime soon, so why don't you just come up here? There's three of them and two of us, so I think we can make the equation work."

"Hey!" A feminine voice protested. "What am I chopped liver?"

Anders turned to their third compatriot, J.D. McNamara, the only female in their group. Though technically this was Damon's bachelor party, one of the groom's conditions was they include one of his best friends since childhood, even if she was a girl.

Currently, J.D. was waving dollar bills at the stripper on the pole. "I know you enjoy the show McNamara, but I didn't think you played for our team. Or are you thinking of taking me up on my offer?" he said with a glint in his eyes.

J.D. rolled her eyes. "If Rogers doesn't want to participate in the fun, you don't have to rag on him. I mean, these poor, hardworking girls could probably use the tips. Do you know Destiny,"—she nodded at the brunette on the left side—"is almost done with her Nursing degree? If you could spare her those dollar bills in your pocket, Anders, she could maybe afford her textbooks next semester."

"Those ain't dollar bills, sweetheart," he said with an impish smile.

Daniel sighed once again and pulled his wallet out of his pocket, taking out half the bills and handing it to J.D. "Here, for Destiny's textbooks," he said before getting up from his chair. The female

"Giving up already?" Anders called.

"Jeeze, stop acting like those clingy girls you kick outta your bed, Stevens. I gotta go to the john alright?" Turning toward the exit, he walked out of the private VIP area and into the main room of the Pink Palace Gentlemen's Club.

Of course, the outside was not much better than the private party rooms, if anything, they were worse. Though it was a "gentlemen's club" there was nothing very gentlemanly about the garish pink, red, and black decor, neon lights, or the various scantily-clad women onstage and the loud, jeering men who cheered them on.

Daniel was no prude, but he just wasn't raised this way. Though he got ribbed a lot because he was polite and nice to everyone—women and women, he didn't pay any mind to the criticisms. A gentleman—a real one—treated everyone else better than they would treat themselves, at least that's what Pops always said. Beau Rogers was old-fashioned in that way and taught his only son the same set of rules he followed his whole life.

He wouldn't have gone to this place or even to Las Vegas except it was one of his good friend's bachelor party. Pops also said that loyalty to one friends' was important, so Daniel felt obliged to come to this weekend getaway, especially since Damon's circle of friends was tiny. Actually, as far as he knew only consisted of the people who came to Vegas. The four men had gone through the Blackstone Rangers training program together and a kind of bond had forged between them. Daniel admired Damon, who had risen up to the position of Chief. Though Daniel himself had been eyeing the promotion, he knew Damon deserved it—he was a natural leader and everyone looked up to him. Besides, there was a lot of responsibility that came with being Chief and he didn't envy the long hours, paperwork, and the bureaucracy that Damon had to deal with. Nope, he was fine being a ranger, as he had been the last five years.

Joining the Blackstone Rangers seemed like the natural career for Daniel. For one thing, his inner Grizzly bear loved the outdoors and the job allowed him to spend most of the day roaming the forests and mountains. And of course, it was in his blood. Before retiring to Texas on his ranch, Beau had been a Ranger for over forty years. It had done his old man proud when he decided to join after graduating from college with his Forestry degree.

Daniel made his way to the men's room, did his business, and then exited. He was making his was through the dark hallway that led back to the main room when he saw two shadowy figures ahead.

"Please ... sir, you can't—" a pleading voice cried.

"I'll do whatever the fuck I want," came the gruff reply. "I'm a paying customer."

Daniel's hackles raised and his inner Grizzly let out a guttural sound. His protective instincts were sounding an alarm and he strode toward the two figures. "Excuse me," he said. "Is he bothering you, miss?"

His shifter vision immediately adjusted despite the darkness and the larger of the two figures—male, of course, stinking of cheap cologned and liquor, whirled around to face him. "Wha— who the fuck are you?"

Ignoring the man, he looked to the woman pressed up against the wall. Much like many of the girls here, she was scantily-clad and her face was caked with makeup, but the wide, frightened look in her eyes made her seem much younger. "S-sir, you should go back to the main floor." The tension and fear rolled off her in waves.

The man's face turned up into an evil grin. "See? Me and Candy here are conducting business. And you should mind your own."

Daniel huffed. "See, normally I do mind my business. But you know what I hate the most?"

"What?"

"I hate bullies." He unleashed the barely controlled anger within him, grabbing the man by the collar and slamming him up against the wall. Candy let out a squeak and turned, dashing away from them.

The man struggled, but it was no use. Daniel's shifter strength allowed up to lift the man off the ground. Opening his mouth wide, he bared his teeth, letting his incisors grow out and his glow with the eyes of his bear.

"What the—" His eyes went wide. "You're one of them!"

He let out an inhuman growl, then dropped the man, who crumpled to the ground. "You bet," he said, looking at the pathetic man in disgust. "Now get the fuck out of here. If I see you approach any woman here—I'm going to hunt you down and make you regret it." Not bothering to look back at the man, he marched out.

By the time he entered the private room again, he and his bear had sufficiently calmed down. In fact, the mask of calm he put on his face belied his earlier rage. He hated losing his temper, but he also couldn't stand it when strong people took advantage of weaker ones. And just because the young woman chose to work at a strip club didn't mean she was fair game.

"You all right?" Gabriel asked as he came over to the buffet to pile a plate high with food.

"Yeah, I'm fine. How's the groom?" he asked, looking slyly over at Damon. The chief's back was turned to them, as he hunched over while fiddling on his phone. "Does he feel as miserable as he looks?"

Gabriel guffawed. "What do you think?"

According to Gabriel, Damon had been strong-armed into this outing, as he didn't want to be away from his mate and future wife, Anna Victoria. Daniel could understand, even though he didn't have a mate himself. His parents were fated mates, so he knew how special that could be. Damon would not only have no interest in any other woman around, but it would pain him to be away from her. "Remind me again why we're here?"

The lion shifter huffed. "I owe Anders a huge favor, okay?

I'll tell you more some other time. But right now, keep him distracted so he doesn't shit on either Damon or me. I promise, this will all be over soon."

Daniel knew the "secret" plan of course, which was one of the reasons he consented to come here in the first place. "All right." Taking his plate of food, he wandered back to the mini-stage in the center of the room and sat down next to J.D, muting on his wings, pizza, and French fries.

About fifteen minutes later, the DJ's booming voice interrupted the playing music over the speakers. "And now we have some special entertainment just for the groom," the disembodied voice of the DJ announced.

The strippers all stopped dancing, picked up their cash from the floor, and disappeared through the curtains at the rear of the stage.

"Hey!" Anders protested as he waved a fistful of bills. "Where are you going?"

"Anders, c'mon," J.D. said as she jumped to her feet. Let's go to the main room."

"Main room? But we were having fun in here," Anders complained.

Daniel followed J.D.'s lead. "Sounds like a plan."

J.D. hooked her arm around the tiger shifter's. "Dude, I think I saw a bachelorette party out there. Bet they're a lot of fun. And looking for some company."

"Really?" Anders's face lit up. "Well then, what are we waiting for? You can be my wing woman, McNamara."

J.D rolled her eyes as she led him out the there, Daniel right behind them. As he followed the two, he couldn't help but feel like someone was watching him. Turning his head, he looked around, but there were too many people around them to just pinpoint anyone looking at him. His grizzly seethed, yowling at him to investigate. Normally, he would have followed his bear's instinct, but they were in a strip club, not deep in the mountains. So instead, he sat next to J.D. at their new table, which was right by the stage.

"Yeah, baby," Anders exclaimed. "Right by the action." He glanced around and saw the group of women at the table next to them, which, based on the crowns and sashes they were, was the aforementioned bachelorette party. "All right! this is better than being trapped inside with those tight asses anyway. Hey baby!" he hollered to one of the women. "Nice tats. They're a piece of art and so are you. Want me to nail you to the wall?"

J.D. roller her eyes. "Cut it out Anders," she said. "They're tryin' to have a good time. Besides, they're not the entertainment." She grabbed his ear and tilted his head toward the stage. "That's what we're here for." She sent an apologetic look to the women.

The lights dimmed as a slow, sensuous beat filled the room. A woman wearing a feather boa entered the stage and everyone clapped and cheered. With another deep sigh, Daniel settled back, arms folding over his chest. *When was this going to end?* Neither J.D. or Anders seemed keen on stopping any time soon. He glanced back toward the private room, where he guessed Damon was finally enjoying his bachelor party. After all, Gabriel did secretly fly Anna Victoria all the way here. And the lion shifter was nowhere to be seen, which meant he probably snuck out. *Lucky bastard.*

"Sir?"

"Huh?" Whipping around, he saw one of the cocktail waitresses leaning over to him, drink in hand. "This is for you."

He glanced down at the drink. It looked innocuous enough; it even had a cherry in it. "I didn't order this."

"One of the girls sent it over," she said. "Candy. She says it's a thank you gift for earlier."

"Oh." It was a nice gesture, but he really didn't need it. "Uhm, can you take it back? Or I could pay for it."

"Oh no." She shook her head. "Please, I couldn't." Before he could protest, she turned on her heel and walked away.

Glancing at the drink, he took a sniff. It smelled like gin and tonic, the flowery bouquet of the liquor tickling his nostrils. However, there was something about it—

A movement caught his eye from the corner of his vision. While everyone had their attention to the stage, someone at the table next to them stood up. He didn't know why, but he just had to look at who it was.

It was one of the females from the bachelorette party. She walked around her friends with an unsteady gait, grabbing onto the back of a chair to steady herself. When she did, she proceeded forward and something about the way she moved made it difficult to tear his eyes away from her.

He took a nervous sip of the drink in his hand, barely tasting the alcohol, his hand trembling as he pulled the glass away from his lips, but his gaze didn't leave hers.

The world around him seemed to slow down, his focus pinpointing on the woman. Continuing forward, she came close to their table, but stumbled forward.

He lunged toward her, grabbing one of her arms before she could hit the ground. She let out a yelp as he pulled her upright, a dark curtain of hair covering her face.

"Are you okay, miss?" Thanks to his shifter reflexes, he didn't even spill the drink in his right hand.

Wobbling on her feet, she brushed the hair from her face. "Yeah, I'm good. Did you—" She stopped as their eyes met. Velvety brown eyes, the color of milk chocolate, widened in surprise.

*Mine.*

*Jesus!*

After that, he couldn't quite describe what happened next—it was kind of like being punched in the gut. But in a good way, if there was such a thing. His bear roared from within him, its massive paws beating at the ground. They had found their *mate.*

"Sorry about that," she said. "Too much to drink ... normally I can handle it but ... special occasion you know?"

"Special occasion," he echoed.

"Well, uh, thanks for the catch," she slurred as she patted him on the arm. "Whoah ... you must work out. Your biceps are like rocks." She gave them a firm squeeze, which made blood rush out of his head and down to ... well, his *other* head. "Er, thanks again."

He watched her pivot on her heel and walk away from him, unable to move or say anything. The room seemed to have quieted down and the only thing he could hear was the pounding of his heart in his chest.

His inner grizzly, however, roared at him and slammed its fists at his insides as if saying, *go after her, you idiot!*

"Shit!" He snapped out of it. *I have to go after her!* She was their mate. But what would he say? Or do? Or how could he explain? Based on her lack on animal, she was obviously human.

Panic rose in him as his bear paced back and forth, probably wishing it could talk. *What would Pops say?* But his mind went blank. *Crap!*

His hand gripped around the glass he was still holding. *C'mon, Rogers, think.* Raising the glass to his lips, he downed the entire drink without thinking. The alcohol ran smoothly down his throat, warming his insides.

*I should just go after her.* His bear agreed, nodding its block head. Slamming the glass down on the table, he strode toward the direction of the restrooms.

*Whoah.*

A wave of dizziness hit him as he made his way to the back

of the room. As a shifter, alcohol didn't stay in his system very long and it took a lot to get him drunk. Did he drink too fast? Or was there something—

His bear growled for attention as it pointed its snout forward. *There she was*, it seemed to say excitedly. Quickly, he caught up to her before she entered the ladies's room, and blocked the door.

"What the hell—oh!" She exclaimed. "It's you."

"Yeah," he said. "It's me ..." Why the heck did his tongue felt like it was going numb?

She straightened her shoulders, and planted her hands on her hips. "Can I help you?"

If she said anything after that, he wan't sure. He couldn't stop staring at her—his mate was gorgeous. Her long, dark hair reminded him of those chocolate commercials where they swirled the dark liquid with caramel. She was wearing a sleeveless dress that showed off her tawny skin and an intricate tattoo of what appeared to be a stained glass wall on her upper arm. And her body ... *damn.* Curves everywhere. It made him want to get on his knees and thank whoever up there deemed him worthy enough to have this Goddess as his mate.

"Hello?" She waved a hand at him. "Dude, are you okay?"

"I am now," he said dreamily. "Now that you're here."

She rolled her eyes. "Uh-huh. What do you want?"

*You. Only you from now on.*

Her eyes went wide. "Excuse me?"

*Crap.* He said that out loud. "I mean, uh ..." God, why the hell was his brain so foggy? Was that an effect of meeting his mate? "I just ... wanted to make sure you were okay. You seemed to be unsteady on your feet."

"Yeah, five vodka cranberries will do that to you," she said sheepishly.

"I know," he lurched forward, backing her up to the other

side, pressing her against the wall. He braced himself with his forearms before he crushed her fully. *Shit, shit, shit!*

"Oh." She didn't protest though, or push him off. In fact, if he didn't know any better, he swore he saw the glitter of desire in her eyes and smell her arousal. "So," she said, her voice low and throaty. "Do you think ... maybe we should, uh, get out of here? Find some fun of our own?"

"I'll follow you to the end of the world if you ask me too, babydoll."

**Blackstone Ranger Hero is available at selected online retailers.**

Printed in the USA
CPSIA information can be obtained
at www.ICGtesting.com
LVHW051638070923
757245LV00004B/480

9 781952 333187